Switchers

'I know about you,' he said. 'I know what you do.'

A cold chill ran up Tess's spine. She stopped and turned back. Kevin was standing still and his face showed the tension he was feeling, but for the first time he was looking her straight in the eye.

'What do you mean?' she said.

The chill spread, prickled through the base of her brain and up into her temples. She was trapped by the intensity of his gaze, and for a moment she was helpless and afraid. Leaves swirled around in the breeze.

'I won't tell,' he said, 'but you must help.'

Switchers

KATE THOMPSON

RED FOX

For Clio and Dearbhla,
my two Switchers

A Red Fox Book

Published by Random House Children's Books
20 Vauxhall Bridge Road, London SW1V 2SA

A division of Random House UK Ltd
London Melbourne Sydney Auckland
Johannesburg and agencies throughout the world

Copyright © 1997 Kate Thompson

3 5 7 9 10 8 6 4

First published in Great Britain by
The Bodley Head Children's Books 1997

Red Fox edition 1998

Printed and bound in Great Britain by
Cox & Wyman Ltd, Reading, Berkshire

Papers used by Random House UK Limited
are natural, recyclable products made from wood grown in sustainable forests. The manufacturing processes conform to the environmental regulations of the country of origin.

RANDOM HOUSE UK Limited Reg. No. 954009

ISBN 0 09 925612 6

CHAPTER ONE

The bus seemed to take hours to crawl through the Dublin traffic. Tess looked out of the window at the passing streets, but she wasn't really seeing them. She was hoping that the boy would not be waiting for her when she got off the bus. She didn't want to have to face him again.

He had been there for the first time on Wednesday, and then again yesterday, and both times he had done the same thing. He had started walking when she got down from the bus, keeping pace with her on the opposite side of the street until she turned into her own road at the edge of the park. She could feel his eyes on her almost constantly, but every time she had glanced across he had looked away. If she quickened her pace, he quickened his. If she stopped and pretended to examine something in the hedge, he stopped as well, always watching. It was almost as if he were teasing her and it unnerved her.

Tess sighed, pulled the band from the end of her french plait and teased it out, releasing her long dark hair from its confinement. It was Friday, and there were two whole days of freedom ahead. She wanted to enjoy the walk home in peace, so that she could make plans.

'Want a piece of chewing gum?' said the girl sitting beside her. Tess smiled and shook her head. In a sense it was dishonest. She would have liked a piece of chewing gum. What she did not want was the embarrassment of someone trying to make friends with her. It was easier to stay out of it from the beginning, rather than face the disappointment which inevitably followed. Because she had been through it too often now to believe that things could ever be different. All her life her family had been on the move. A year here, two years there, following her father's promotions wherever they took him.

Tess had found it difficult at first but she had come to accept it as the years went by. Her parents encouraged her to make new friends wherever they were, and had even gone as far as arranging parties for her, but they didn't understand. They couldn't. She went along with their parties and sometimes went as far as to invite someone home for a weekend, to please them. But it was the best she could do. She had long ago come to realise that she would never really be able to make close friends. She was different and that difference was something that she would never be able to share with anyone.

The girl beside her got up as her stop approached. 'Bye,' she said. 'See you Monday.'

'See you,' said Tess. There were still a few girls, like this one, who were making an effort, but it wouldn't last long. Soon she would be forgotten and ignored, dismissed as a swot or as too stuck up to bother with. That was painful sometimes, but it was easier than having to pretend to be like everyone else.

The bus stopped and the girl got off, pulling on her gloves. Students from the local vocational school were about on the streets. They didn't have to wear uniforms, and they looked relaxed and human compared to the girls in her school with their matching gaberdines and hats and shoes. Tess had wanted to go to the vocational school instead, but her parents said they wanted the best for her. She might have put up a stronger protest, knowing that they felt guilty about moving yet again, but she couldn't argue too hard. She had already used up all her influence insisting that they get a house beside the Phoenix Park. It had been vital. She could not have survived in any other part of Dublin.

The city traffic was always at its worst on a Friday evening, but at last the bus reached her stop and she got down, and walked a few yards along the main road. It was bitterly cold again and she cursed herself for forgetting her scarf. This freak weather had been going on for some time now, and there was no excuse for forgetting. She pulled up her collar and braced herself against the icy autumn breeze.

As she turned off the main road into the tree-lined avenue which led to her road, she groaned inwardly. He was there, leaning against the wall, waiting for her. There was no one else about. Tess walked quickly, looking firmly down at the ground. Today she would not be drawn. She would not look over and give him the satisfaction of catching her eye. She watched the paving stones intently and said to herself: 'He doesn't exist. If I don't look at him, he isn't there.'

But he was there, and today he was more there than ever. Out of the corner of her eye she saw him crossing over the street towards her, pushing his fair hair away from his eyes in a gesture that was already becoming familiar.

Her first instinct was to run, but she knew that it would be useless. She was strong, despite her small and wiry frame, and given the right circumstances she would be hard to beat over a short distance. But today she was wearing narrow shoes with heels, part of the ridiculous uniform, and her schoolbag was heavy. If he wanted to catch her she wouldn't have a chance and if he didn't, if he was just trying to unnerve her, then he would have succeeded, and she would look and feel a fool. So she carried on walking, but looked determinedly away from him, towards the houses.

He walked on the very edge of the footpath but even so, Tess moved in towards the walls and hedges they were passing, as far away from him as possible. The street seemed endless.

'Cigarette?' he said.

'No.'

'Ah. Don't smoke?'

'No.'

'Very wise.'

Tess glanced at him. He was holding a very crumpled pack from which he extracted an even more crumpled cigarette. She noticed that he had no gloves and wondered how he could bear to have his hands out in the cold. In the brief instant that she looked at him, he caught her eye with a sly, sideways glance. His eyes were slate grey and very hard. They gave her butterflies.

Tess raised a hand to her hair, aware that it was

still crinkly from the pressure of the plait. 'What do you want?' she said.

'Oh, nothing much,' he said. 'What's your name?'

'None of your business.'

He stopped, abruptly, to light his cigarette, and quite automatically, Tess stopped too. She caught herself and went on again immediately, but it was too late. He would take it as a sign of acceptance and encouragement, and that was the last thing she wanted.

The strange weather was bringing an early autumn to the country. Leaves swirled in the wind, many of them still green. Even with her fleece-lined gloves and thick tights, Tess was feeling the cold. The wind stung her cheeks, giving them a colour that they usually lacked. She stuffed her hands into her armpits as she walked.

The boy caught up with her in a few strides, light-footed in his worn trainers. For a while he said nothing, puffing at his cigarette, concentrating on getting it going. Tess sneaked a glance out of the corner of her eye. He wore an army parka, frayed around the cuffs, and a pair of dirty jeans with holes in the knees. He was older than she was, fourteen or fifeen perhaps, but he wasn't any taller. If he was going to give her any kind of trouble she thought she could probably hold him off until someone came out of one of the houses. Assuming they did. But what could he possibly want with her, anyway? Money? He certainly looked as if he was short of it.

'It might be, and it might not,' he said.

'What?'

'It might be my business and it might not.'

Tess glared at him and he looked nervously away.

'Your name,' he went on. 'Mine is Kevin. Or Kev. Take your pick.'

'No thanks.'

He laughed then, a high-pitched, musical laugh. Suddenly, Tess had had enough. She stopped in her tracks and turned on him, no longer uncomfortable, just furious.

'What do you want?' she shouted. 'Why don't you just leave me alone?'

He jumped and stopped dead. Tess took advantage and walked quickly away, but he caught her up. They were getting close to the edge of the park where Tess's road began.

'Don't be like that,' he said. 'I just want your help, that's all.'

'Well you can't have it,' she said, more confident now that she had turned the tables. 'I don't have any help to offer.'

The corner drew nearer. She would soon be home.

'Perhaps you do,' said Kevin, walking closer now, and Tess thought she detected a hint of urgency in his voice. She noticed that he seemed to be constantly glancing around him, as though he was afraid of being seen. She wondered if he was on drugs, or if the police were after him.

'If you want help so badly,' she said, 'you should ask my father.' As she spoke she heard herself using a tone she despised, the snooty little rich girl, the spoiled brat. But she couldn't stop herself. She turned towards him, her dark eyes taking on an expression of disdain, and said: 'Or shall I ask him for you?'

They were at the corner. On both previous days the boy had parted from her there and turned in the opposite direction. She knew he wouldn't follow her.

But as she made to swing around the corner, he caught hold of her arm. She shook herself free, but he darted round and stood in front of her, his hair flopping into his eyes again.

'Wait,' he said.

She stepped aside and went past him.

'And what if I told your father about you?' he said.

A cold chill ran up Tess's spine. She stopped and turned back. Kevin was standing still and his face showed the tension he was feeling, but for the first time he was looking her straight in the eye.

'What do you mean?' she said.

'I know about you,' he said. 'I know what you do.'

The chill spread, prickled through the base of her brain and up into her temples. She was trapped by the intensity of his gaze, and for a moment she was helpless and afraid. Leaves swirled around in the breeze.

'I won't tell,' he said, 'but you must help.'

Tess turned away. 'I haven't the faintest idea what you're talking about,' she said.

CHAPTER TWO

On Saturdays it was traditional for Tess to go shopping with her parents. It was supposed to be the high point of the week, to wander around whatever town they were in, buy what they needed and have a slap-up lunch at the best restaurant they could find.

Tess's parents often spoke about money being short, but Tess didn't really know what that meant. She knew only that from time to time she was embarrassed by the fact that she was one of the better-off girls in her school. Her father was hard-working and well paid. If there was something that Tess wanted, she generally got it.

On the whole, however, she didn't want all that much. Her parents saw her as a quiet child, perhaps too quiet, who was given to reading in her room after school and taking long walks in the countryside at weekends. During the holidays they saw little of her. She would set out on her walks after breakfast, whatever the weather, and return when she felt like it, often quite late, though seldom after dark. She didn't talk much about these walks, but her parents were proud of her knowledge of nature and in particular of wildlife. The last house they had lived in was on the edge of a small town in the south-east. It had faced out into the open countryside, but backed on to the built-up area. Tess had loved it there. The park was a poor substitute, but it was better than nothing.

For Christmas one year her parents had bought Tess a bicycle and often she set off cycling instead of walking. They had offered her riding lessons, too, with a view to buying her a pony of her own, but she had declined. 'Ponies are such fun,' she had said. 'I couldn't bear to sit up on top of one and boss it around.'

So they had dropped the idea and left Tess to her own devices. They saw no reason to do otherwise because she seemed, despite her lack of friends, to be quite content with life. When they learnt of the imminent transfer to Dublin, they both knew that it was going to be hard on Tess, but even so, they were unprepared for the strength of her reaction. She burst into tears when they told her, and locked herself away in her room. When she came out, she refused to speak to them at all for several days, and her mother came as close as she ever did to losing her temper about it. Instead, as usual, she became angry with Tess's father, and the house was full of slamming doors with bristling silences in between.

Eventually, Tess capitulated and agreed to move to Dublin on condition that they get a house either on the outskirts or beside the park. It wasn't easy, but they managed it. It was just as well, because Tess would have gone out of her mind if she had been made to live hemmed in by houses. Her 'walks' were the only thing that made the difference between happiness and misery in her life.

On that particular Saturday, her father had some work to do and told her that they would not be going into town before mid-day. Tess hid her delight. Now she would have the morning to herself. An unexpected bonus.

'All right if I go for a walk, then?' she said.

'Are you sure?' her mother asked. 'It's bitterly cold out.'

'I'll wrap up,' said Tess.

She put on jeans and her new puffa jacket, hat, scarf and gloves, and went outside. The wind wasn't strong, but it was colder, if anything, than the day before. Tiny particles of ice drifted in it, not quite snow yet, but a warning of it.

Tess looked up and down the road. During the summer holidays, there wasn't a parking space to be had for miles along the edge of the park, but today there were few cars. One or two stalwart owners were walking their dogs, and a few determined-looking families were playing soccer or frisbee, but mostly the park was deserted. In particular, to Tess's relief, there was no sign of Kevin. If he wasn't there today, the chances were that he hadn't been there on other Saturdays either. And if he hadn't, then he couldn't have followed her to the secret place she had found, and he couldn't have seen what she did there.

She began to relax a little as she walked across the bare fields of the park. She had always been careful, after all, very, very careful. It was vital that no one should see her and she had always made sure that they didn't. Kevin had just been bluffing. It was a clever bluff, too, because what teenager has not done something in their life that they would prefer their father not to know about? But a bluff was all it was, she was sure about that. If he tried again, she would invite him to come home with her and see what he had to say to her father. There was no way he would come.

She felt better, even light-hearted, as she came to the rough part of the park where her place was. Sometimes, when people were around, it was a little awkward getting in there without being seen, but today there was nobody within sight at all.

It was an area of small trees, ash and elder, with plenty of brambles and other scrubby undergrowth to provide cover. Tess looked around carefully. A woman had come into view, walking an Irish wolf-hound which bounded with graceless pleasure across the open space of the park. Tess knew how it felt. She had tried a wolfhound once.

To be extra safe, Tess walked around her favourite copse and peered into one or two of the neighbouring ones as well. Well trodden paths ran between them all, and there was always a chance that somebody might be approaching, hidden by the trees. She stood still and listened for a long time. She knew the ways of the birds and small creatures well enough now to understand their voices and their movements. There was nothing to suggest that anyone apart from herself was making them uneasy.

She looked around one last time, then slipped into the copse. It was a place where she would not care to come alone at night. Even in broad daylight it was dark in there, and a little eerie. There were light paths through it that were clearly used quite often, and scattered here and there throughout the undergrowth were fast food wrappers and empty cans and bottles. Tess went on towards the middle, standing on brambles which crossed her path and ducking beneath low branches until she came to a place where the trees thinned a little. Here the undergrowth had grown up taller and thicker because of the extra light. A long time ago, a fairly large tree had fallen here, and the brambles had grown up around its remains. The smallest branches had rotted away, but the bigger ones were still intact and made a kind of frame.

Tess looked and listened one last time before she stooped and crawled into the narrow passage which led into the dark interior. Once inside, she was completely hidden from human eyes by the dense growth of brambles which covered the carcass of the tree. When she came out, she was a squirrel, full of squirrel quickness and squirrel nervousness, darting and stopping, listening, darting again, jumping.

Everything and anything in life was bearable as long as she had this. What did it matter if she had to wear that absurd uniform and go to that snooty school? At the weekends she could be squirrel, or cat, or rabbit, or lolloping wolfhound or busy, rat-hunting terrier. What did it matter if that vain and hungry boy was pestering her, trying to scare her? What did he know of the freedom of the swift or the swallow? What did he know of the neat precision of the city pigeon, or the tidiness of the robin or the wren? She would call his bluff and let him bully someone else. But just now, she would forget him as she forgot everything when she was squirrel, because squirrel hours are long and busy and full of forget-fulness.

The sun poked through the branches above, and if it wasn't the warm, autumn sun it might have been, it still didn't matter so much. Its bright beams added to the dizzying elation of scurrying about and jumping from branch to branch, and Tess was too busy to be cold.

Squirrels do as squirrels must. It didn't matter that she would not be there to hibernate during the winter. Autumn was collecting time, so collect is what she did. But because she wouldn't have to eat her store of foodstuffs in the winter, it didn't particularly matter what she collected. Some things, like rose hip seeds and hazel nuts, seemed urgent, and could not be resisted. She stuffed the pouches of her cheeks and brought them to her den. Other things, like sycamore wings and the mean, sour little blackberries that the cold, dry autumn had produced, were less urgent, but she brought them anyway because they looked nice, and there wasn't anything else in particular to be done. If the other squirrels found her habits strange, they were too busy with their own gathering to give her their attention. The only time they bothered about her was when she ventured too far into someone else's territory, and then a good scolding was enough to put her right.

She knew most of the other squirrels. Earlier in the year, before school started, she had often spent time playing with them, engaging in terrific races and tests of acrobatic skill. She always lost, through lack of co-ordination or lack of nerve, but it didn't matter. It was sheer exhilaration to move so fast, faster than her human mind could follow, and to make decisions in mid-air, using reflex instead of thought. She remembered some of those breathtaking moments as she encountered particular squirrels, but there was no time for that kind of thing now. Life was rich with a different kind of urgency. Food was going to be scarce this year.

There was a clatter of wings in the treetops. For an instant the thicket froze like a photograph, and then its movement began again. Nothing more than a grey pigeon making a rather clumsy landing. Tess caught a brief glimpse of something shining on the ground and swooped down a tree trunk head first to investigate. At first she thought it was a ring pull from a drinks can, but as she got closer she saw that it was a real ring, a broad band of silver, scarcely tarnished at all. The metal grated unpleasantly against her little teeth, but she was determined to have it. She took a firm grip on it and pulled, but it would not come. A sharp blade of tough grass had grown up through it and become entwined with other grasses on the other side. She tugged again, and all at once was aware of another of those sudden woodland silences which always spell a warning.

She froze. She could see no enemy, but she smelt him, and he was close, very close. It was a smell she had never encountered before. She looked around carefully, and found herself face to face with the strangest squirrel she had ever seen. He was small and strong, his ears were sharp and pointed, and he was red, with black and white stripes running down his back. Every other squirrel in the copse was still, looking down at this oddity.

'He's not a squirrel at all,' thought Tess. 'He's a chipmunk. What on earth is a chipmunk doing in the Phoenix Park?'

As quick as any squirrel, the chipmunk darted forward and took hold of the ring in his teeth. As though reassured by this, the other squirrels relaxed and went back about their business. But Tess was infuriated. Whatever he was, wherever he came from, he was not going to have her ring.

She sprang forward and took a grip on the ring beside him. It may have seemed like a courageous thing for her to do, to take on this intruder, but she was supported by the knowledge that if she were in real danger all she had to do was to change back into Tess. Not only would she escape, but she would give her enemy the fright of his life.

Only once, so far, had she needed to do it, and that was when she had been a rabbit at dusk, not far from their last house. A fox had appeared from nowhere, and she had fled with the other rabbits towards their burrows. But the chap in front of her had been slow to get in, and the fox had been just about to close his teeth on her thigh. Instead, he was brought up short by a human leg, and he ran away home extremely frightened and bewildered.

She had been lucky. There had been no one around to see it happen. It was a last resort, but here in the darkness of the thicket she was prepared to use it if she had to.

But she didn't. As soon as she took hold of the ring, the chipmunk released it and used its teeth instead to cut through the tough grass. The ring came free, and Tess raced off along the thicket floor, holding her head high so that the ring would not get snagged on plants or fallen twigs. The chipmunk followed. At the door to her den, Tess dropped the ring and scolded him soundly. He backed off some distance and sat on the stump of the fallen tree, watching her with a sly gleam in his eye which was disturbingly familiar. Tess picked up the ring and marched in through the tunnel entrance, then went into the deepest corner of the bramble patch and dropped it there behind a big stone. But when she turned round, she found the chipmunk right behind her, watching every move she made. She sprang at him, chattering and scolding as loudly as she could, and he bolted away towards the light at the tunnel entrance.

Tess turned back to find another hiding place, but no sooner had she done so than he was there with her again, his tail high behind him, darting this way and that, always just out of reach of her teeth. For all the world he was behaving like a young puppy who wanted to play.

Tess stopped haranguing him and watched. Perhaps chipmunks weren't busy gathering at this time of year? Or perhaps he had escaped from a zoo or a private collector, and didn't know what he was supposed to be doing. Cautiously, she followed him. When she reached the end of the tunnel, he bounded off and leapt half way up the trunk of a tree, and then down again. He raced back to her, and then off again, into the branches this time, tempting her, teasing her. And why not, she thought, why shouldn't she play? There was no need for her to be gathering. She followed, slowly at first, so that he still went ahead and came back, until she gained confidence and ran up beside him. Now they were off, speeding along together through the trees and across the open spaces between them. They went from thicket to thicket, exploring them all at the highest possibly speed, and from time to time they raced out onto the open part of the park, running and jumping through the tangled grasses as far as they dared, then returning helter skelter to the safety of the trees.

Tess gave herself over completely to the game and the joy of companionship. It happened occasionally that she met a friend of a sort in the animal world, but as with human friends, it always seemed to be hard work. This was different. The chipmunk was as eager for company as she was. This time it was he who had found her and asked her to play. She couldn't remember when she had last felt so happy, and she didn't try. There was only now, the perfect moment, and it went on, and on, and on.

Until, suddenly, Tess caught sight of the sun. She had forgotten why, but she knew that it was much further across the sky than it ought to be. She stopped on a branch, her whiskers twitching, trying to quieten her flighty little squirrel brain so that she could think. All that came into her head were nuts, and a strong and compelling need to return to her den.

She raced pell mell back to the copse and the fallen tree. The chipmunk followed, still trying to play.

As soon as she was in the den, she remembered. The trip to town. She didn't know the time but she knew that it was late, very late. Her parents would be anxious. They'd be angry, too, and probably quarrelling. The chipmunk had followed her into the den. With all the squirrel fury she could muster, she turned on him and drove him out. He hovered at the door looking perplexed, but she sprang at him again, chasing him further away. Then she raced back into the darkness and, before he had time to follow her, she made the change. As she crawled on her hands and knees back out of the den, she expected to see him running away in terror, but there was no sign of him. None at all.

Halfway home across the park Tess realised that she had forgotten the ring. She sighed. It would be there again tomorrow. If she wanted something to worry about, she need only look ahead.

CHAPTER THREE

When Tess arrived home, breathless and contrite, her mother said: 'Never mind. If your father hadn't been working this morning, none of this would have happened.'

Her father stayed silent. He had become engrossed in an international football match on TV, so Tess and her mother took the bus to the centre of the city and had tea together in Bewley's. Afterwards they split up to do a bit of shopping. Tess spent some of her pocket money on a book about rodents which had a whole chapter on chipmunks, and the rest on a huge bag of sunflower seeds.

When they got back, Tess went upstairs and lay on her bed intending to read the rodent book, but she was so exhausted by her squirrel adventures that she fell asleep and didn't wake up until her father called her down for dinner. During the week the family ate formally around the dining room table, but quite often at weekends they relaxed in front of the living-room fire with trays on their knees. Tess sat down in an armchair and picked up her knife and fork. Her parents were watching a soap opera on the TV, but it was one that she found boring. Her mind wandered, back to the first time she had Switched and discovered that she did not always and evermore have to be just Tess.

She had been quite small, just seven or eight, and she had woken unusually early on a summer's morning because she was uncomfortably hot. There were images in her mind of a strange dream that she had been having, but they vanished before she could capture them. She sighed, and it seemed to her as she did so that time had slowed down. The sigh took for ever, both coming and going, as though there was room in her lungs for more air than she had thought.

Outside, the birds were singing unusually loudly, and the sun was streaming through a gap in the curtains and on to her bed. She realised that this was probably why she felt so hot, but when she lifted her hand to throw back the covers, something brown and furry jumped up on to her chest.

Tess was not a screamer, even at that age, which was probably just as well. If she had attempted to scream at that moment, the noise would have woken half the street, and everything might well have been ruined. Instead she stayed motionless for a long, long time, waiting for the creature to show itself again. When it did not, she began to relax a little. Whatever it was wasn't all that big, and surely she would be able to frighten it away. Slowly, carefully, Tess sat up. As she did so, she could see that the furry thing was still there on the top of her quilt. In slowly dawning horror, she realised that it was not a small creature, but the paw of a very, very large one. She swung round, expecting to see the rest of the beast crouching on the floor beside her bed, but there was nothing there. And as she turned back, she knew. She lifted her hand, and there was no hand, just the great, brown paw lifting to her face to feel the long snout and the round, furry ears. Tess had turned into a bear.

For a long time she stayed still. She had read about such things in fairy tales. They were usually caused by wicked spells or curses laid by witches or evil fairies. Tears of hopelessness rolled down her hairy cheeks and spilled on to the quilt, making a dark patch that widened and widened. She listened to the birds, wondering how they could seem so joyful when she felt so sad. She might have stayed there indefinitely, weeping a great stain into the quilt, were it not for the fact that bears find it uncomfortable to lie on their backs for so long.

Her fingers would not work properly. The quilt snagged in her claws as she tried to push it off, but she managed to get herself disentangled and scrambled down on to the floor. It was surprising to find how comfortable a bear can be, and for a while she just ambled here and there around the room, getting accustomed to her strange limbs.

After a time the sound of the birds and the fresh scent of the morning drew her to the window. On the third attempt, her clumsy paw caught the curtain and hoiked it to the side, and she stood on her hind legs and leant up against the windowsill, blinking in the bright light. The smell, the sound, the feeling of the fresh air in her nostrils was so delicious, it was almost magical. She was filled with delight at being a bear and she stretched her nose up towards the cool gap where the window was open. Just at that instant, however, she caught a scent, and then a glimpse, of the paper boy cycling down the road.

As quickly as she could, Tess dropped back to the floor and away from the window. The horror of the situation returned. What on earth was going to happen to her? From the room beside hers, she heard her parents' alarm clock ringing, and put her heavy paws up to her ears in dread. Any minute now she would hear her father padding along to the bathroom to wash and shave, and then he would pop his head around the door and say, 'Rise and shine,' or, 'Show a leg.' Sometimes he came in and drew the curtains. Sometimes he even sat down on her bed and chatted for a while before he went down and put on the kettle. But what was going to happen now? What would he do when he saw, instead of his girl, a brown bear?

He was humming now in the bathroom as he shaved. Would her mother be more likely to understand? If she looked her carefully in the eye, would she recognise her own Tess?

Tess shambled miserably around the room, feeling huge and heavy and clumsy. As she went by it, she knocked over the dolls' house. The crash it made as it landed scared her, and she jumped and knocked over the Lego. It scattered across the floor and as she walked the sharp edges hurt her paws.

The bathroom door clicked shut. Tess heard her father's footsteps in the hall. She sat down in the middle of the room and prayed with all her might to be a little girl again.

The door opened. 'What's all the noise about?' said her father.

Tess sat still and looked carefully up towards the door.

'What have you been doing?' her father said, as he came into the room.

Tess stared at him in astonishment. How could he not have noticed?

'Are you all right, sweetheart?' he said, squatting on his heels beside her.

She stared wide-eyed into his face, then looked down at her hands. She was Tess again, sitting on the floor in her nightdress, all warm and pink and human.

'I was a bear a minute ago,' she said.

'A bear!' said her father. 'Well. No wonder you made such a mess.' He righted the dolls' house and began putting the things back into it.

'But I was, Daddy, I really was.'

'Well, you'd better be a tidy little squirrel now and pick up all that Lego before your mum sees it. You can pretend they're all nuts.'

'But I wasn't pretending!'

'Of course you weren't.'

'Do you believe me?'

'Of course I do.'

But she knew by the tone of his voice that he didn't. Changing into bears just wasn't the kind of thing that adults did. They would be far too worried about what other people were thinking. So when, a few weeks later, Tess turned herself into a cat, she promised herself that she would never, never tell anyone ever again. And she never did.

That boy, that scruffy Kevin character, he couldn't know. He just couldn't. It wasn't possible. All the same, there was something about the way he had looked at her that scared her and made her almost believe that he did, somehow, know what she could do.

'Tess?'
'Yes?'
'You're not eating your dinner, sweetheart.'
'Oh. I was just listening to the news.' She hadn't been, but she did now.

'Meanwhile,' said the TV newscaster, his face impressively grave, 'the freak weather conditions continue. The snow storms that have been ravaging the Arctic regions for the past eight weeks show no signs of abating, and their area of activity continues to increase. The death toll in northern Europe now stands at more than seventeen hundred, and there are many more people unaccounted for. Evacuations continue across the Northern Hemisphere.'

The TV screen showed a picture of a line of cars driving through a blizzard.

'Inhabitants of Alaska and northern Canada continue their southwards exodus as weather conditions make their homes uninhabitable. Air-rescue teams are working round the clock to move people from outlying areas, and snow-ploughs are working twenty-four hours a day to keep the major routes clear. However, it is feared that there may be thousands of people trapped in snowbound vehicles on minor highways throughout the area, with no hope of relief from the already over-stretched services.'

'There's something fishy about all this,' said Tess's father.

'Fishy?' said her mother. 'How can there be something fishy about the weather?'

'I don't know, but it isn't natural.'

'How can the weather not be natural?' her mother asked. 'If the weather isn't natural, what is?'

'Well, it's not normal, anyway.'

'Normal is a different question entirely. No one is saying this is normal.'

'Shhh!' said Tess.

'The fourth land attempt to reach the weather-bound Arctic drilling station has had to be abandoned,' said the newscaster above pictures of army snowmobiles and tanks. 'Radio contact with the rig was lost soon after the storm conditions began, and successive attempts to reach it by air and by land have failed.'

An army officer appeared on the screen, dressed like a Himalayan mountaineer. Snowflakes whirled around him.

'It's just impossible out there,' he said. 'Conditions like these have never been encountered before. The temperatures are falling off the bottom of the thermometer and visibility is nil. With the best will in the world, it is not feasible to expose army personnel to conditions like those.'

Tess thought he looked scared.

'I still say it's fishy,' said her father.

Her mother sighed in exasperation. Tess stood up with her tray. 'I'm going upstairs to read,' she said.

'Don't you want any pudding?' said her mother.

'No, thanks.'

'It's lemon meringue pie.'

'I'm not hungry. Perhaps you could leave me a piece for later?'

Tess took the tray out to the kitchen and went back up to her room. No one was saying it, but it was on everybody's mind. If those snowstorms continued to spread, it would not be long before they closed in on

Ireland, as well. And then what would it matter if that stupid boy did or didn't know her secret?

CHAPTER FOUR

In a private office in the Pentagon in Washington DC, the same army officer who had made an appearance on Tess's TV was sitting at a table with several other men. One was his chief of staff, General 'Whitey' Snow, and another was the chief of staff of the airborne forces, General Wolfe. The others were ministers and advisors from the American government. There were no members of the public or the press among them.

The officer, whose name was Colonel Dale 'Big Daddy' Dunkelburger, got up and wandered restlessly across the floor for a minute or two, then took his seat again in a leather chair at the head of the table. On a trolley at his right hand was a large, square tape recorder and, in front of him, covering most of the tabletop, was a huge map of the Arctic Circle.

Colonel Dunkelburger sighed and rubbed his eyes.

It had been a long time since he had slept, and it looked like being another long time before he would again. With an expression of grim resignation, he glanced across the table and nodded at General Snow.

The General stood up and cleared his throat. 'Gentlemen,' he said, 'the matter we are here to discuss today is one of the utmost seriousness and gravity.'

There was a murmur of assent from the assembly.

'Now,' the General went on, 'I know that all of us here are signatories of the State Secrets Act, and I know that you are all aware that the seal on the door of this office binds you to that oath. Even so, what Colonel Dunkelburger is about to reveal to you is so important that I want you to take another oath now, a personal oath, on whatever you hold most sacred, that what you are about to hear will not pass beyond these four walls, even if you might believe yourself that such secrecy is incorrect.'

One of the President's advisors shook his head and sighed.

'General,' he said. 'We all appreciate that there's something here that you consider to be pretty important, but don't you think that maybe you're being a little melodramatic about this? Most of us here have to deal with State secrets every day, and I reckon the oath we've all taken has been good enough so far.'

'I appreciate your point of view, Mr Dunwoody,' said the General. 'But I believe that when you hear the evidence that we have on these tapes, you may understand. We're talking about an issue of global importance here, as opposed to state security, and I believe that it might unleash a world-wide panic if it

27

were to become public knowledge. I have no intention of calling the Secrets Act into disrepute, but it might not be sufficient in this case to cover all eventualities. I hope you can understand that and appreciate that no disrespect is intended.'

Dunwoody nodded and, one by one, somewhat self-consciously, the assembly rose and swore their own personal oaths. When they were finished, Colonel Dunkelburger reached into the inside pocket of his jacket and produced a small tape which he fed into the machine beside him.

'This, gentlemen,' he said, 'is the last message that our Arctic Surveillance station in North Alaska received from the polar drilling rig, a week after it was marooned by the storms. I think it's worth saying at this stage that we have no reason to believe that this transmission was received by anybody else apart from ourselves.' He switched on the machine. The reception was poor and full of crackling static but nonetheless the voices could be heard.

'Yeah, boys, we're still OK here.' It was the voice of a young man, a bit of a wiseguy, but putting a brave face on a difficult situation.

'Nothing to report?' said the radio officer.

'Yeah, a lot to report. A hell of a lot. But it's all snow, you know? A hell of a lot of it.'

'How's the platform holding up?'

'I guess it's OK. The winds are as high as ever, though. There's a lot of creaking and groaning going on, it's pretty scary sometimes, but I don't think there's been any more damage since last Tuesday.'

'You still got plenty of supplies?'

'Yep. We're having a ball, you know?'

'So morale is OK?'

'Good enough. We – ' Here there was a loud bang. 'Whoops! Someone in a hurry with the coffee.'

Now there were excited voices in the background, but none of it was picked up clearly by the radio mike apart from the louder exclamations. 'But it's massive, man!' and 'I swear to God it's moving.' Then the young man came back to the mike. 'Hey, I gotta go for a minute. The guys are kind of worked up. Cabin fever, I guess. I gotta go and take a look. Will you hold on to the line there for a minute?'

'Sure, Chris. But what's happening?'

'I'll get right back to you. Don't go away, now.'

There was a long pause, during which nothing could be heard except the hiss and crackle of static. Around the table, the listeners shifted in their seats as the tension mounted. Then there was a second bang, like the first, followed a moment later by a series of loud metallic groaning and grating sounds, and then there was nothing. The radio connection went dead.

Colonel Dunkelburger took the tape out of the machine and slipped it back into his pocket. 'We don't know any more than you do, gentlemen,' he said, 'and that isn't much. We have had no radio contact with those guys since. Any kind of air rescue is impossible in those conditions, as General Wolfe will confirm.' He looked towards Wolfe, who nodded sagely, and then continued. 'We have gale-force winds out there which are whipping around and back every couple of minutes. Nothing can fly accurately enough in there. And as you know, we sent in land teams, but those have failed as well.'

'Why don't you tell everybody why, Colonel?' said General Snow.

'Yes, sir. Uh, these were unsuccessful for a number

of reasons. The first two teams turned back because the snowmobiles they were using were too light and were just getting thrown about in the winds out there. The third team took specially modified machines which could handle the winds a little better, but we didn't have our back-up system worked out well enough and we couldn't keep the fuel supplies up. It gets pretty dangerous to run out of fuel in those conditions as I'm sure you can all appreciate, because no fuel means no heat, and without heat nobody can last long out there, believe me. It's cold. We got a couple of cases of frostbite, and we were lucky that it wasn't worse.'

'And the fourth team?' asked the presidential advisor.

'The fourth team was doing pretty well. They had top quality vehicles fitted with special heaters and back-up power supplies in case of emergency. We had teams running well to keep them supplied up front with food and fuel, and a shift system in operation. They had been on the route for three or four days.' He stood and leaned over the map, pointing to a dotted line which ran a short distance across it. 'We had our main supply depot here in Barrow, in Northern Alaska, which is about six hundred miles from the drilling station. The pack ice is hard right up to the shore these days, so we could send the expedition right out on to it. The leading members of the team had reached here, which is about four hundred and fifty miles from the rig.'

He reached into his other inside pocket and took out a second tape, exactly like the first, which he slotted into the machine.

'There were two 'mobiles out ahead,' he said, 'each with two men. The rest of the team were on supply runs and the nearest ones would have been a mile or so behind them. We're tuned into car two, here. Car one was off the air.' He sighed and wiped his forehead with the back of his hand. 'I'm sorry about this, gentlemen, but I don't want to hear this any more than you do, believe me. And you had better hang on to your chairs.' He switched on the tape.

This time the line was a lot clearer. 'Still moving along,' said a young man's voice. 'Ground's pretty level. Harry's taking a nap.'

'No, sir,' said Harry. 'Just resting my eyes as per orders.'

'Yeah,' said the first voice. 'It's tough on the eyes all right. Got little white worms running across mine. How come I can see white worms when everything else is white?'

'They got black edges?'

'Let me see. Yeah. I think they got black edges.' He laughed. 'But the little b. . . . .s won't keep still and let me look at them.' There was a pause, then the same voice continued. 'Any news your end?'

'Nope. Everything's pure white and deadly boring.'

'Oh, well. At least we're not missing – Hey! Woah! What the hell is that?'

'What's up?' said Harry. 'Hey! Stop, Bud.'

Bud's voice was suddenly full of terror. 'We are stopped, God damn it. It's that thing that's moving!'

'Mother of Christ. It's alive!'

There was a single scream that sent a chill of horror through the whole room, and then the radio went as dead as the first one. The silence spread to the listeners. After a long time, Colonel Dunkelburger cleared his throat.

'We never regained contact with that car or the other one. I called off the mission immediately and brought the team back home as quick as I could. The way the weather is worsening, we can't maintain the base in Barrow any longer, and we've pulled all our men out of the area. I guess I should say here that we have no plans to make any further excursions into the region as long as current weather conditions continue.'

The Secretary of State broke into the silence which followed.

'If I can just try and clarify things, here,' he said. 'Are we to understand that there's something living out there in the middle of those storms?'

'I can't say, sir,' said Colonel Dunkelburger. 'We have no more evidence than what you have just heard.'

'But surely you have all kinds of intelligence at your disposal? You have instruments for detecting heat sources, don't you?'

'Nothing that could be accurate enough to pick out a living entity in storms like those. Besides, our experts tell us that no living species within our current spectrum of knowledge could survive on the surface in those temperatures for more than a few minutes.'

'So what are you suggesting?'

General Wolfe broke in. 'With due respect, Mr Secretary, we didn't come here with the purpose of suggesting anything. We came here because we thought that the evidence on those tapes should be made available to the Government.'

'Well,' said the Secretary. 'It goes without saying that you guys have the full backing of this Government to take whatever investigations or action that you think necessary.'

'That's much appreciated, of course,' said the

General, 'but I'm afraid there are no further investigations we can take. This country has three armed forces, but in these conditions, every one of them is blind. We're overflying the area constantly with all kinds of aircraft, armed and unarmed. We have every kind of surveillance equipment trying to get a look at what's happening in there, but we're not getting any information at all.'

'As I see it,' said Dunwoody, 'you're telling us there's a possibility that there are some kind of alien creatures inside those storms and there's not a thing you people can do about it?'

'We're not trying to tell you anything, sir,' said Colonel Dunkelburger, 'but the conclusion we have reached is pretty close to that, yes.'

There was another thoughtful silence, and then General Snow said, 'I think perhaps now you will understand the need for absolute secrecy.'

The next morning, Tess slept late and had a leisurely breakfast. The mood in the house was low, and Tess knew that it was not just because of yesterday's mix-up. Even her father could not raise his customary Sunday spirit.

It was this weather. There was no change, and the radio reports gave no indication that there was likely to be. The meteorologists admitted that they were baffled. Satellite pictures revealed nothing except what everybody already knew. The Arctic storms were as active as ever, and were gradually spreading southwards. There had been no rain since the day it all started, and now the radio gave the first warnings of possible water shortages. It wasn't yet necessary to introduce rationing, but people were being asked to reduce their consumption as much as possible.

The whole business made Tess gloomy. She was still a bit tired, too, from her wild antics of the previous day. But she wrapped herself up as well as she could and set out across the park with the sunflower seeds under her arm.

The scene was similar to the day before. Only those who refused to be defeated by the weather had made it to the park, and they were few and far between. Tess wound her scarf around her face and breathed through the wool. From time to time she jogged for a while to keep warm.

When she got to the wooded area she opened her bag and wandered through the thickets, scattering sunflower seeds as she went. She listened to the sounds of the birds and small animals, and laughed a little at their mixture of suspicion and delight. When the bag was empty, she checked the surroundings carefully and went quietly into her den.

Tess was completely adept at changing now. It had taken a lot of practice, and when she was younger there had been times when she couldn't make it work. It required a state of mind that was somehow more, and somehow less than just thinking. First, she would need to know what she wanted to be and have a clear picture in her mind of whatever creature it was. Next, and more difficult, she would have to try and imagine how it felt to be that creature from the inside. Then she had to let go. Letting go was the most difficult part, because the moment of changing was a bit scary. For that moment, brief though it was, it felt as though her mind was dissolving, and everything around her became vague and fluid and insubstantial. Once that moment had passed, everything was fine again. She took on the being of whatever she had become, and they were all as solid in their own way as her customary human existence. But there had been times, in the past, when she had failed to change because she had shied away at the last moment from that frightening instant of dissolution, and clung to what was certain and safe.

More recently she had discovered that thought, concentration and anxiety were all hindrances to the process of change. For several years now she had dispensed with them and simply plunged, spontaneously, into any shape she fancied. In the dark of previous dens, Tess had experienced the nature of most of the wild and domesticated creatures in Ireland, and most of the more common birds as well. She knew now, beyond all doubt, that she could be anything she wanted to be.

As soon as she was a squirrel again, Tess set out in search of the chipmunk. There was no sign of him in the immediate vicinity, so she scampered in the trees and hunted through the branches. But it soon became hard to keep her mind on what she was doing. All the other squirrels were frantic with activity, gathering the sunflower seeds she had scattered and bringing them home to their nests. For a while she resisted the temptation but in the end it proved too strong for her. She knew that she had brought those seeds and she knew that she had no need to make a winter store, but the instinct of a beast is strong, and soon Tess gave in and joined them.

It filled her squirrel heart with joy to find food so plentiful. She filled her little cheeks until they bulged, and scurried back to her den time after time. All around her the other squirrels and the birds and the fieldmice were delighted by the unexpected windfall and Tess knew that her pocket money had never been better spent.

Still there was no sign of the chipmunk. Every now and then Tess would remember him and take a leap up into the treetops to see if she could see him from up there. Then she would go back to work and forget him again.

The day drew on and Tess had a fine heap of sunflower seeds in her den. She realised that it would soon be time to go home, and it was then that she thought, for the first time, of the silver ring. Hurriedly, she unloaded her cheeks and skipped across to the dark corner where she had left it. The stone was there, big and solid, and she searched around behind it, but there was no sign of the ring. Tess sat down and thought as hard as a squirrel can think, but both squirrel mind and Tess mind were sure that she had left the ring just there, behind the stone. She searched again and, when she still didn't find it, she searched all the corners of the den, pushing aside the rotten leaves and twigs with her nimble squirrel fingers and feeling around where it was too dark to see. All at once she knew that the chipmunk had taken the ring. She stopped still and tried hard not to believe it but she knew that it was true. He had been such a friend, such a good friend, but now he had let her down, by taking her ring and disappearing. It filled her heart with such sadness that she didn't want to become Tess again, because she knew that most of the creatures of the earth feel sadness from time to time, but only humans collect it like a store of nuts and feel the need to make it last.

But she had to be herself again. There was homework to be done for tomorrow, and then another week of school before she could be here again, and free. She changed before she had time to think about it. With a human hand she reached behind the stone and felt around carefully, but there was no doubt now that the ring was gone. The little heap of sunflower seeds which had seemed so huge and satisfying to her squirrel self looked small, now, and pathetic. She brushed them into the palm of her hand and scattered them on the floor of the thicket as she set off for home.

CHAPTER FIVE

Monday dragged on, as always. Tess had brought her rodent book to school, and read it secretly beneath her desk during maths and religion, but since the disappearance of the ring it had lost its appeal. There were no references to wild chipmunks in Ireland, or any suggestion that chipmunks had any interest in collecting baubles.

The other girls in Tess's class had come to accept that she preferred to keep herself to herself. She knew that it would be hard to make up all that lost ground if she ever changed her mind and wanted to make friends, but she had created an image for herself in the school and for the moment she was content to leave things as they were. But that evening, when a photocopied letter was handed to each girl to bring home to her parents, she rather wished that she was free to join in the celebrations that followed. The letter read:

'Dear parent,
       Owing to the prevailing weather
conditions, the girls will not be required to
wear school uniform until further notice.
       Yours sincerely,
              M.L. Harvey (Principal).'

Tess almost got off the bus at the stop before her own. She knew that there had to be a way through to the park from there, and once she had reached it, she couldn't go wrong. She pictured that stupid Kevin's face as he realised she wasn't on the bus. He could stand there and freeze for all she cared. But at the last minute, Tess's courage failed her. She might well freeze herself if she got lost and had to wander around the streets for too long.

She hoped that he wouldn't be there, but he was, on her side of the street this time. He was leaning against the wall with his hands in his pockets, watching for her. She noticed that his face brightened for an instant the moment he caught sight of her, but then it took on the familiar, shifty expression. Tess thought of crossing the street, but she knew it was useless. Instead she looked straight ahead and walked briskly past. Kevin fell into step beside her.

After a minute of strong silence, he said: 'Ready to tell me your name yet?'

Tess swung around and faced him. 'Look, why don't you just clear off and leave me alone!' She was shouting louder than she meant to, and a woman on the other side of the street gaped at them as she passed.

Kevin looked away, to hide the apprehension in his face. After a minute or two, he said: 'What kind of manners are those for a young lady?'

'What would you know about manners?' said Tess. 'With your whinging and scrounging.'

'Scrounging?' said Kevin.

Tess walked on, and he followed.

'Who's scrounging?' he said.

'What are you doing, then, if you're not scrounging?'

Kevin sighed deeply and took out a cigarette. 'You're being ridiculous, you know,' he said.

'Listen who's talking! I've already told you I don't want anything to do with you. You're not getting my name and you're not getting any money, either. If you want to get something, then get lost.'

Kevin laughed. 'That's a good one,' he said. 'Did you think of that one on the spot?'

Tess didn't know whether to be infuriated or flattered, and when Kevin stopped and turned to the wall to light his cigarette, she almost stopped as well. But she didn't get caught out this time. Instead she quickened her pace, almost to a run. Kevin caught her up. 'You won't help, then?' he said.

'No.'

'But you don't even know what I'm asking you for.'

'Whatever it is I haven't got it. And if I had I wouldn't give it to you.'

'But you have got it. In fact, you're the only one who has.'

'Rubbish.'

They were walking so fast now that they were nearly at the edge of the park. Suddenly, Kevin dodged in front of Tess and blocked her way. She tried to sidestep, but he threw away his cigarette and grabbed hold of her shoulders. She was shocked at the sudden movement, and surprised by his strength, but it was the look on his face that stopped her from trying to break away. There was no slyness there now, no fear. He was looking at her straight on, and his eyes were bright and keen and completely serious.

'Is it really possible,' he said, 'that you haven't worked this out yet?'

Tess tried to think of something clever to say, but she couldn't. For some reason she knew it wasn't the time for being clever. Kevin spoke slowly, as though she were a rather dim child. 'Do you really believe that there are chipmunks in the Phoenix Park?'

Tess felt her mouth drop open. Her mind flew back to Saturday. She had been so careful. It was impossible that he had seen. He took his hands from her shoulders and blew on them to try and warm them. Tess remained motionless, open-mouthed, staring. Kevin put his hands in his pockets, and the sly gleam returned to his eye. And just as she remembered that same look in the bright little eyes of the chipmunk, Kevin took hold of her gloved hand and dropped something into it.

It was the silver ring.

Tess was afraid that her emotions would show on her face. All those years of silence and secrecy and guilt were over, and she was no longer alone. She would almost have hugged Kevin then, despite his scruffy clothes, but he began to talk before she had the chance.

'You'll help, then?' he said.

Tess was bewildered. 'But how? What?'

'I'm not sure, yet,' said Kevin, gazing out across the park. 'But if you meet me tonight we'll find out.'

'Meet you? Where?'

'Connolly Station. One o'clock.'

'One o'clock?'

'Is that too early?'

'Too early?'

'Use your head,' he said. 'You'll have to get out, won't you? And you'll have to get there.'

'But I can't,' said Tess. 'How can I?'

Kevin blew on his hands again and shrugged. 'If you can't, you can't,' he said, and he began to walk away. 'But I'll be there anyway.'

She watched him as he went. She knew nothing about him, nothing at all. Then she remembered the little chipmunk racing with her, playing, staying close, and she felt that she did know him, at least as well as she needed to.

'Kevin?' she called.

He turned back. 'Yes?'

'My name is Tess.'

He smiled and gave her a thumbs up. But her heart was heavy as she walked towards her house. How could she possibly do as he asked?

CHAPTER SIX

Tess lay awake, listening to her parents getting ready for bed. She could hear their voices through the wall, but not the words. From the tone of their conversation she could tell that all was well with them, and the house was relaxed and comfortable as long as they were content. But it didn't make Tess any happier.

Kevin had asked her for help and she had let him down. The clock on the wall said twelve twenty-five. Even if she had the courage to cross the city at this hour, there was no way she could do it. The last buses would be on their way out of the centre of town and they would not be bringing passengers back in. A taxi, even if she could find one, would be too expensive. If she had meant to be there, she would have left an hour ago or more. But it was impossible. Couldn't he understand that? What parent would allow their thirteen-year-old daughter out in the dead of night to meet a boy they had never set eyes on?

If she had any friends in the area, she might, just might, have pretended to be staying with them. If she had gone with someone to a disco or a film, she could have risked her parents' alarm by going on from there and coming back late. But there was no one for her to go with and nowhere to go. She couldn't even sneak out. Just ten minutes ago her father had put his head around the door and listened, as he did every night. She had made her breathing as deep and regular as she could. It was dreadful, being an only child.

Twelve thirty-five. Poor Kevin. He would be there, soon, all alone among the homeless people and the winos, looking round for her, waiting. And here she was, lying in her comfortable bed, wretched, feeble, worthless.

She turned over on to her side, but she knew she wouldn't be able to sleep for a long time. The clock on the wall ticked with infuriating monotony. Outside, an occasional car passed along the road, and in the tree opposite a barn owl began to call.

Tess listened, slightly calmed by the familiar sound. It seemed strange tonight, different somehow. Her nerves were on edge. She sighed and turned again in the bed.

'What a fool,' said the owl. 'What a foo-ool.'

Tess sprang up, almost before she understood why. Of course! She would have laughed and shouted out loud if she hadn't been afraid of waking her parents. As quietly as she could, she opened the window and climbed up on to the sill. The freezing night air blew into the room. She wouldn't be able to close the window behind her, but it was too bad.

A moment later, a barn owl was speeding towards the centre of the city, high above the houses and offices. It was a young owl, healthy and strong, and singularly delighted by the power of flight.

Tess knew Connolly Station well. Although they had lived in Dublin for less than three months, they had often visited the city in the past to do some special shopping or to go to a show or a play, and as often as not they had come by train.

It was easy enough for her to find the station from above. The city was spread out like a map beneath her, and once she had found the railway lines where they crossed the North Strand, she could not go wrong. The difficulty would be finding somewhere to land and change her shape without being seen. But her attention was drawn from the problem as she flew down over the station, because she was joined by another owl. It swept in from somewhere above and behind her, and as it drew level it bumped into her and knocked her off balance, so that she fluttered wildly in the air for a moment or two. As soon as she was steady again, the other owl returned to fly beside her. Tess was afraid that she had broken some territorial rule and offended the other bird. It would not be a problem if it allowed her to fly away, but she was afraid that if it continued to be aggressive she would either fall or be forced too far away from the station to get to Kevin on time.

But it didn't collide with her again. Instead it flew alongside for a while, then moved a little ahead and veered across her so that she had to swing to her right. As soon as she did so, it dropped back beside her and turned its head carefully to look at her. It was then that Tess realised it was Kevin, and if an owl could have smiled, she would have done. Instead, she nodded her head in recognition, and he blinked three times, then flew on ahead. She followed as he swept over Busaras and the Custom House, then swung away from the river and back towards the north side. They followed streets which became darker and narrower until they came to a few blocks of dilapidated flats built around dark, rectangular courtyards. Above the first of these they flew in diminishing circles until they were sure that no one was around, then Kevin dropped into the courtyard and swooped straight in through an open window on the second floor. It was a lovely piece of flying. Feeling slightly reckless, Tess let go and followed.

By the time she had got her bearings in the room, Kevin had already turned back into human shape. Tess followed suit. As an owl, with her good night eyes, she had seen him quite clearly, but for a girl, the dark in the room was almost impenetrable. For a moment or two, she was quite unnerved. The place smelled bad, of mouldy mattresses and soot and stale beer. But there was something even worse.

'Kevin?' she said.

'Yes?'

'Can you see me?'

'Not really, no.'

'I'm in my pyjamas.'

She heard his laugh ring out around the room. It was hard and scornful, and it hurt.

'Shut up,' she said. 'I didn't have to come here, you know. You don't know what it cost me to get here.'

'What did it cost you?'

But she didn't tell him, because then he would know that it mattered to her not to let him down. Instead she said, as unkindly as she could: 'Is this where you live, then? Is this your house?'

He struck a match and lit a candle and a cigarette from it. 'I don't live anywhere,' he said.

'Don't be stupid,' said Tess. 'Everyone lives somewhere.'

'Who's everyone?' he said.

Tess shivered. In the candlelight she could see the stained mattress in one corner, surrounded by a jumble of newspapers and empty tins and bottles. There was an untidy heap of dark blankets in another corner, but Tess would not have touched them, let alone put one around her shoulders.

'Do you live here?' she asked. 'Seriously?'

'Of course not!' Kevin sounded bitter. 'What do you think I am?'

'Where do you live, then?'

'I already told you that.'

'Then who does live here?'

'No one. Some old tramps use it sometimes, when they can't get into the hostel.'

The cold was beginning to hurt. Kevin didn't seem to be aware of how bad it was. By the flickering light of the candle, she could see him looking from one corner of the room to another with that familiar nervousness. She was suddenly close to tears.

'What are we doing here?' she said. 'I don't understand any of this. How am I supposed to help you?'

Kevin shrugged. 'I'm not even sure myself, yet,' he said, 'but I know it's important. There's a rumour going around. The rats want to bring me somewhere.'

'Rats!'

'Yes. You got something against rats?'

Tess had. A rat was one of the things that she had never been and had no desire to be. But before she could say anything, Kevin went on.

'A rat is about the best thing to be in a city like

47

this. They have the run of the place, you know? They never go hungry.' He smiled at the distaste clearly evident on her face. 'They have a lot of fun, too. More often than not I'm a rat.'

He watched closely for her reaction. Tess tried not to show it. The idea filled her with unease. For although she had spent a lot of her time being all kinds of other creatures, she had never considered herself to be anything other than human. But if Kevin spent most of his time being a rat, then what did that make him? It made sense of the way he behaved when he was human, though; his nervousness, the sense that she had when she was with him of there always being an enemy somewhere close at hand.

'Never been a rat, huh?' he said.

'No.'

'Don't worry. You'll enjoy it. But there's quite a stir going on about this cold weather. At least, I think that's what it's about. Everybody's suffering, you know, not just the people. That's why I came looking for you. They want me to meet somebody. I don't know who it is, but it's a long way.'

As Tess watched him, the tense expression left his face, and there was a momentary confusion in his eyes as he said: 'I didn't want to go there on my own.'

There were suddenly too many questions. There was too much to share with this strange boy, and possibly too much to cope with. And it was too cold to face any of it.

'I have to go home,' said Tess. 'I have to get warm and think it over.'

'But there's no time to think it over. This thing is important, Tess. This weather's getting worse all the time.'

'Do you think I don't know that? Don't you realise I'm getting frostbite standing here?'

Kevin bit his lip. 'I'm sorry,' he said. 'I wasn't thinking.' He began to take off his coat.

'Don't be ridiculous,' said Tess. 'What difference does it make if you freeze instead of me? The point is, the whole thing sounds ridiculous to me. How can we possibly have any effect on the weather, whatever we do?'

'I don't know,' said Kevin, zipping up his parka again, 'but I do know this. Most of my life I've been going in and out of the animal world, and never before did they take any particular notice of me. But now they have. They know that I'm different and they're asking me for something.'

'I'm totally confused, Kevin,' said Tess, 'and I'm too cold to think straight. I have to go home.'

'But we can go straight away,' he said. 'Come on. You won't be cold once we get moving.' As he spoke, he was pointing towards a large hole in the skirting beside the fireplace.

'As a rat?' said Tess.

'Of course.'

Tess shook her head, and at the same moment changed back into an owl. She hopped out of the window and flew straight up and away towards the park. Gradually the activity warmed her and she began to feel better. The whole idea was crazy. All she wanted to do was to curl up in her own bed and forget all about it. But she was not allowed to. As she landed lightly on the edge of her bedroom window, she realised that Kevin was right behind her.

CHAPTER SEVEN

Kevin and Tess stood in her room, facing each other.

'Goodnight, Kevin,' said Tess.

'Oh. You're going to bed, are you?'

'Yes.' She wanted to close the window on the night and all that was in it and allow the room to warm up, but she couldn't do that until he was gone. Instead, she climbed into bed and wrapped the covers around her.

Kevin wandered round the room, examining her things. It made Tess uncomfortable. It always made her uncomfortable when someone less well off than she was came to the house. She had no pride in her standard of living, and in situations like this she felt rather guilty.

'You've got a lot of books,' said Kevin.

'Observant, aren't you?'

'Have you read them all?'

'Most of them.'

He took a thick volume out of the book case and opened it. 'You like mythology, then?'

'My dad does. He buys most of that stuff.'

'Do you read it?'

'If I'm bored enough.'

Kevin leafed through the book. 'This is a good one,' he said. 'I haven't seen this one before.'

Tess sighed and tried to drop him a hint by turning her face to the wall, but he went on: 'I spend hours in the library, you know.'

'Oh? When you're not rummaging through people's dustbins?'

She couldn't see him, but she could imagine the look on his face in the brief silence before he said: 'Yes. Or raiding their kitchens or waking up their babies at night. Rats are OK, you know, you shouldn't underestimate them. They have their own codes of behaviour, even if they're not like yours. They have a language, too.'

'All animals do.'

'No, not really. All animals have ways of communicating, but the rats actually have a language, a sort of visual language.'

Tess said nothing, and after a while, Kevin went on: 'I love all this stuff, though, all those heroes and gods and wonderful beasts. It's the best thing about people, if you ask me. Their imagination.'

'I didn't ask you,' said Tess, and as soon as she had said it, she regretted it. It was just one step too far.

Kevin hurled the book across the room. It hit the wall above her head with a loud crack and landed on the pillow in front of her nose. She sat up in bed.

'For God's sake, Kevin!' she said, as loud as she dared. 'You'll wake my parents!'

'Your parents? Your precious mammy and daddy? Who cares? Eh? As long as you're all right, all warm and cosy with your feather duvet and your central heating and your own private little life. The rest of the world can go hang, can't it, as long as you're all right, Jack!'

'Shh, Kevin, don't shout! I don't know what you mean, can't you understand that? I don't understand what you're asking me to do.'

'Nor do I!' said Kevin. 'But I know that it's important. And even if it isn't, I have to find out.'

He came over to her and sat on the edge of the bed. Tess's nerves were on edge, waiting for the sound of her father's feet in the hallway.

'You have to help me, Tess,' Kevin went on. 'You just have to. I can't do this on my own. For one thing, I don't have very much time left.'

'What do you mean?'

'It doesn't go on for ever, you know, this thing, this ability we have. Did you know that?'

'No.'

'Only until we're fifteen.'

'How do you know?'

'Someone told me. She was one of us, too, but now she isn't. She learnt it from another Switcher. After her fifteenth birthday she couldn't change any more. That's the end of it.'

The news came as a blow to Tess. She had always believed that her gift would be with her for the rest of her life, the one thing she could be sure of.

'We all meet someone who tells us,' said Kevin, 'and we all meet someone we have to tell. I don't know how it works or why, but it seems that it always does. Anyway, the point is, I'm nearly fifteen, you know? And I'm nervous about what's happening.'

'So you want me to come along and hold your hand?'

Kevin looked crestfallen, and suddenly Tess didn't know why she was putting up such a resistance and being so unkind. She lay back on the pillow to think about it, and Kevin sat quietly, glancing at her from time to time in his nervous, sideways manner.

Tess realised as she lay there that there was nothing to think about. If she refused and sent him away, she would never know what it was about and whether her gift had given her a part to play in some scheme or other. She would have to live with that uncertainty for the rest of her life. No matter how crazy it seemed, she had to go. There was no choice.

She sighed and threw back the covers. A look of delighted surprise crossed Kevin's face. He turned away quickly so that she wouldn't see it, but she could still see the way he felt by the spring in his step as he crossed the room. She pulled on her jeans on top of her pyjamas, and then two sweatshirts, a thick jumper and two pairs of socks. Then Kevin waited in her room as she crept downstairs, feeling like a burglar in her own house, to get her down jacket and gloves.

Back in the bedroom, Tess hesitated. Whatever anxiety she had about the risk she might be running for herself was nothing compared to the feeling that gripped her now. For some reason she knew beyond any doubt that she would not be returning to that room before morning, and that her parents would have to face the shock of coming in and finding it empty. She felt sick, but there was no longer any question of turning back. With hands that trembled more from tension than from cold, she searched through the drawers of her desk for some notepaper that her aunt had given her for Christmas. The she sat down and picked up her pen.

The paper had delicate impressions of swans in blue and gold. Kevin leaned over her shoulder as she wrote. 'Nice paper,' he said.

'Shh.'

'Dear Mummy and Daddy,' she wrote. 'I have to go away for a little while. I'm sorry, but I can't explain to you why. But you must trust me, just this once. Don't send anyone to search for me. It would only be a waste of time. I promise that I will take care of myself, and you must promise me that you will do the same and not worry too much. I will be back as soon as I can. Love you with all my heart, Tess, XXXXXXXX'

'Yuck,' said Kevin. ' "All my heart." '

Tess swung on him. 'Shut up,' she said, in a vicious whisper. 'Shut your filthy mouth. Just because you haven't got anybody.'

He shrugged and turned away, and Tess was sorry, because she realised for the first time that it was true. He had nobody. Nobody at all.

She pinned the note to her pillow and took a last look round the room. Then, side by side with Kevin, she walked to the window.

The two owls swept away again over the city. Kevin led the way back towards Connolly Station, but instead of returning to the flats, he headed for a small patch of wasteland in the same area, where houses had been demolished to make way for some new building project which had never materialised. They overflew it once or twice, checking out the area, and then they began to descend.

There was a crowd of young men gathered around a car a couple of blocks away, but they were not close enough to be a danger. The owls flew a little lower over the wasteground again and, to Tess's horror, her sharp night eyes saw that the whole area was swarming with rats. There was a high chain-link fence around the plot, but nonetheless the local people had managed to turn the place into a dumping ground for their rubbish. Mainly it was large things, old couches with the stuffing hanging out, broken TVs and fridges and mattresses with bulging springs. But there were black plastic bags there as well, spilling out their contents of empty tins and vegetable peelings and tea bags. A perfect breeding ground for rats.

As the owls spiralled cautiously downwards, there was a sudden flurry of rapid movement as the rats leapt for cover, and then there was nothing. Absolute stillness. Into this, the two birds landed, and before Tess could even take a breath, Kevin had dissolved before her eyes and become a rat.

It was strange to watch it happening. If Tess had been asked, she probably would not have been able to describe what it looked like, because it looked, in a sense, just the way it felt. She had the same dizzying sensation of the world losing focus and becoming fluid, as though the observer also were drawn into the process of change and somehow became part of it. She watched as Kevin trotted away a little distance, then stopped and looked back. Tess stood still, with her wings folded, looking around her with large eyes that missed nothing, even in the darkness. The rats were everywhere, poking their noses out of the tin cans and paper bags and carpet folds where they had taken cover. Kevin sat up on his tail and twitched his whiskers with that same nervousness that carried into his human form. Tess wanted to be with him, but she was stuck. She just couldn't bring herself to make that change.

It wasn't only as a human that she hated rats. Every creature that she had ever been hated them, too. The birds hated them because they would raid any nest they could reach and whisk away any hatchling or fledgling that got out from under its parent's eye. Cats and dogs hated them because they were thieving and provocative, and because if they were hungry enough they would take even a young pup or kitten from its bed. Other scavengers hated them because they were greedy and aggressive and invariably got the better of an argument. Even the large and tolerant beasts like horses and cattle found rats distasteful, because they respected neither peace nor privacy, and they fouled whatever fodder they were unable to eat.

Kevin came back towards her. The other rats, sensing that she was not a threat, had begun to emerge from their hide-outs. She turned her head slowly from side to side. She was not afraid. An owl is a match for any rat. She watched them carefully, allowing her owl instinct to savour the idea of snatching the plumpest of them and bringing it away with her to the nearest tree. But it was not to be. From the street came the soft click-click of a dog's claws on paving stones. The rats froze. As Tess watched, the dog appeared at the wire and stopped, looking straight at her. For a long moment, nothing moved. Then the dog, with a single, soft bark, announced its intention and ducked through a gap in the fence.

Looking back, Tess could never understand exactly why she made the decision she did at that moment.

It would have been as easy, and probably much safer, to lift off into the air and fly away from the scene, but she didn't. The sudden danger resolved her deadlock, and an instant later she was running for her life behind Kevin's retreating tail and leaping for the safety of a dark hole in the side of an upturned couch. Together with several other rats, they wormed their way between the springs and stuffing into the safety of the deep interior. From there they could hear the dog sniffing and scratching at the torn fabric, but they were quite confident that he couldn't reach them. Sure enough, he soon became bored and gave up. The rats wasted no time. Before he was out of sight down the street, they were out in the open again.

Suddenly, Tess found her mind full of vivid and disturbing images. The owl in the dog's mouth with feathers flying. Herself as a rat being shaken in his teeth, and the horrifying sound and sensation of her spine snapping. She stood transfixed, trying to clear her mind, until Kevin caught hold of her by the whiskers and gave them a tweak. It was then that she remembered what he had said about the rat language, and she realised that he had put those images into her mind. He was angry. But before she could work out how to answer him, they were approached by another rat, and then another, and her mind was fully occupied by their expressions and the images they were passing.

'Here among us, you two, huh? Days and nights, days and nights, us lot listening, looking, huh?'

Tess was surprised at how well she understood them.

'You two sleeping, huh? Days and nights, days and

57

nights. Stuffing fat bacon, huh? Trying to make a family, huh?'

Tess was shocked, but Kevin was angry. He jumped on the rat who had suggested it and bit his ear until he squealed. 'Ear gone, nananananana! Sit down, calm, days and nights, you two, empty streets, empty skies.'

Kevin was giving images now. 'Long canal, long towpath. Us two, many streets.'

Tess was grateful that he didn't let them know that the delay was largely her fault. 'Many streets, many streets,' she thought, 'yep,' and she was surprised when the others nodded and twitched their whiskers.

'Yep, yep, many streets. Many streets behind, many streets ahead, move, run, little old lady sitting beside a fire, looking you two, listening you two, run, huh?'

And run they did, straight away. Across the waste-ground and down a hole which led under the foundations of the neighbouring house and through a series of underground passages lined with brick, earth and rubble.

Kevin went ahead with the rat whose ear he had bitten. The other stranger ran along beside Tess, watching her cautiously with what she interpreted as a rather stupid grin. From time to time the passageway grew narrow and the lead rat and Kevin would fall into single file until they were through. But Tess's companion didn't seem to understand. If she gained speed to go ahead, he gained speed as well, and if she slowed down to drop behind, he also slowed, all the time looking at her with that same, stupid expression. They survived a couple of tight squeezes, but managed to become completely stuck at one particularly narrow spot.

'Oops,' said her guide in rat language. 'Narrow, narrow. Us two, oooh, very, very thin, huh? Squeeze.'

Tess scrabbled with her claws and they managed after a brief struggle to break free. They ran on, and made up some of the ground they had lost. It was quite dark down there beneath the houses, and Tess realised that she was acting by an unknown sense which wasn't sight. She was aware of the spaces around her and the way the tunnels changed ahead and behind, even though she could actually see very little. After a while, they emerged into the open space of a basement, where light flooded through a grating from a lamp post on the street above. The rats stopped and looked around cautiously, before scuttling together across the empty space, which seemed huge after the narrow tunnels. At the other side they formed a line again to slip through a hole in the corner of the floor. Kevin was ahead of Tess and as he disappeared she noticed that his right hind foot had only three toes. But before she had a chance to wonder about it, her companion was back alongside her.

'Long nose,' he said.

'Huh?'

'Long nose.'

They were approaching another tight gap, and this time Tess stopped and thought as clearly as she could of the two of them going through it quite sensibly and politely, one at a time. But to her annoyance, her guide stopped as well, and said again: 'Long nose.'

She made a sprint for the hole, but he was too quick for her and there was no doubt that they would have got stuck again if Tess hadn't stopped in time. He grabbed hold of her whiskers and pulled her round to face him. She could just see the outline of his face in the darkness.

'Long nose,' he said, and he caught hold of his own nose and pulled it. She noticed for the first time that he did have an unusually long nose.

'Long nose,' she said, and was pleased to find that sarcasm was a readily available quality in the rat language. 'Yep, yep. Sunny days, happy rats, long nose. Me through the hole, you through the hole behind me, huh?'

He wrinkled his nose. 'Yep, yep,' he said, and she darted through before he had time to change his mind.

Kevin and his friend were waiting, but ran on when they saw the other two coming.

'Long nose,' said Tess's companion yet again.

Tess was beginning to get really fed up. 'Long nose,' she said. 'Small brain.'

'Huh?'

Tess mimicked his grin. 'Long nose, happy you, happy me, huge sack of oats in a big barn with no cats.'

'Nanananana. Long nose. You, huh?'

'Short nose.'

'Nanana. Short-nosed rat in a hotel basement, many many streets.'

At last Tess understood, and she felt slightly foolish. Long Nose was his symbol, his mark, his name in the visual language of rats.

'You, huh?' he said again.

Tess was at a loss. Her name was meaningless in this world. There was no way to translate it. And as far as she could tell, she was a completely ordinary rat with no outstanding features at all. Her mind searched for images, but none of them seemed suitable.

'Owl, huh?' she said at last.

'Nanana,' said Long Nose. 'Nanananana. Owl carrying off young rats, us rats sad, us rats angry.'

There was another narrow opening ahead, and this time Tess managed successfully to communicate the idea of single file. She ran ahead of Long Nose into the dark gap, and was surprised to find that it stayed dark and narrow. It was sludgy and slippery underfoot, and there was a strong smell of drains. She waited for the tunnel to broaden out, but it didn't, and it soon began to seem as though it never would. Tess began to feel claustrophobic. The only reassurance was the sound of Kevin's pattering feet before her, and those of Long Nose behind. Gradually the smell grew stronger, and Tess realised that it was more than just drains. It was sewers. The stone passage they were in was sloping downwards now, and Tess found herself beginning to slither on the slimy stuff beneath her feet.

'This is the most foolish thing I've ever done,' she thought to herself. 'What on earth am I doing here? How could I have allowed myself to be talked into this?'

She had no time to dwell on it, however, because the next moment Kevin flashed her an image of a rat wearing a parachute, and then they were falling through the air in the darkness.

CHAPTER EIGHT

They landed with a splash, a shock of cold water that made Tess gasp and splutter. But she found that, before she knew it, she was swimming, and quite strongly too. For someone who had never swum before, either as a girl or any other creature, it was pretty exciting and completely took her mind off the nature of the liquid they were travelling in. There was just enough light for her to see the shapes of the other rats ahead of her and she swam up close beside Kevin before Long Nose had a chance to move in and monopolise her again. Kevin looked across and acknowledged her with a brief nod. His eyes sparkled and she caught the image he gave her of an underground train speeding along beneath a huge city. Then he gave her a second one, of four rats going twice as fast through their own underground system. If she had known how, she would have laughed.

Before long, the four of them came to a wider

canal, and they swam with a gentle current until they came to a shoal of sludgy stones and trapped paper, which allowed them to climb out of the water and into another system of pipes and drains.

Tess was beginning to get tired. The drains seemed to go on for ever, always sloping gently upwards and always wet and slimy underfoot. It took all her strength and concentration to keep close to Kevin, who seemed to find the going no problem, and the whole business was made worse by the irritating presence of Long Nose, who trod on her tail at every possible opportunity.

She called in Rat to Kevin: 'Boy and girl, out in the open, deep breaths, sleeping.'

He called back: 'Boy and girl squashed in drain-pipe. Spaghetti.'

By the time they emerged, quite suddenly, into the cold, clear air, Tess was so exhausted that she felt she couldn't travel another yard. She wanted badly to be human, at least for a while, but before she could repeat her request to Kevin they were off again. They had come out on to another piece of waste ground which lay between two huge warehouses. Tess followed the others out on to a wide street. There was no sign of people or dogs, but they stuck to the deepest shadows all the same, running in single file close up to the walls and sprinting across the open spaces in between. At the end of the street lay the river. Ships were tied up beneath cranes, waiting for loading or unloading, but there was no activity now. All was still and silent.

The fresh air had given Tess a second wind and she was comfortable enough now as the little group followed the warehouse walls parallel to the river for several hundred yards. There were lights here, and they were much more exposed to possible danger than they had been in the drains, but Tess was happier nonetheless. The others, however, did not relax until they left the warehouses behind them and crossed through the wire fence which surrounded an area of huge coal heaps. Then they slowed their pace and picked their way among the loose slag at leisure.

'Dawn,' said Kevin, dropping back beside Tess.

'Happy us,' said Tess. 'Boy, girl, sitting on the coal, huh? Boy smoking cigarette, huh? Talking, huh?'

'Us four sleeping,' said Kevin. 'Curled together, warm.'

It was not an image that appealed to Tess, though it clearly did to him. She was still not entirely comfortable about being a rat and, besides that, it would be the first time that she had allowed herself to sleep as an animal. It was an idea that had always scared her a little, not only because she might sleep longer than she meant to and arrive home late, but because sleeping was a kind of forgetting and she was afraid that she might not remember who she was when she woke up.

Kevin nudged her with his shoulder and wrinkled his nose. Then he darted on ahead and, resigning herself, Tess followed.

The four rats slept throughout the day in a snug and well concealed hole beneath a portakabin at the entrance to the coal-yard. It was far from being a sound sleep, because the floor above their heads was walked on almost constantly, and the sounds of men's voices filtered through the wood. Lorries passed in and out all day, their tyres crunching on the coal dust, alarmingly close. But Tess didn't mind. Rat dreams were strange and frightening and it was a relief to be woken from time to time and to be able to remember where she was and why. Sometimes Kevin woke with her and they would exchange a few images and touch noses for comfort before they went back to sleep. Sometimes the rat with the bitten ear woke too and moved in small, irritated circles, trying to get comfortable again. Long Nose, it seemed, didn't wake at all, but snored and sighed throughout all the coming and going in ignorant contentment.

The best sleep came in the three or four hours between the closing of the yard and the arrival of darkness. Those hours passed like minutes but refreshed the four rats better than any before them. They spent a few minutes cleaning themselves when they woke, then emerged, bright-eyed and sleek, into the strange, orange gloom that covers cities at night. A few flakes of snow were falling, but there was little wind, and the rats were in no danger of getting cold as long as they kept moving. They were hungry, though, and Tess was about to discover that the hunger of a rat bore no relation to any hunger she had ever known. It began as a warm and rather pleasant sensation which made her feel energetic and strong, but within an hour it had grown larger and more demanding, and her feeling had changed to one of enormous courage and pride. She was sure that she would have stolen a bone from a dog at that moment, and longed for a chance to prove it.

'Eat, huh?' she blasted at Kevin.

He jumped at the force of her message but answered calmly: 'Basement, dark, black bags, flash restaurant, a few streets.'

Tess held on to the image of the diners in their expensive clothes, taking their time over their food. Her parents brought her to that kind of place from time to time, but she was sure that Kevin would never have been in one, at least not while he was human. She decided that she would bring him out, when all this was over. She had her own account in the post office, and she would buy him some new clothes, if he would let her. It was a pleasant fantasy. She would be on familiar territory. He would be on edge, worse than usual, but she'd make him feel at ease and make sure he got the best the restaurant had to offer.

'Long Nose.'

Not again. Tess almost squeaked in annoyance. She was tempted to use the pent-up urgency of her hunger to jump on him and box his ears, but just in time she realised that he was probably hungry, too. By now they were back among the rat runs that honeycomb the foundations of the city, and Tess had allowed herself to fall back behind Kevin again and into the company of Long Nose.

'You, huh?' he said.

Tess was as stuck as before. To make time, she said: 'Him, huh?' and sent an image of the rat with the chewed ear.

'One black whisker.'

Tess hadn't noticed. 'Him, huh?' she said, indicating Kevin.

The image that came back was a disturbing one, an awful random mixture of rat features combined with the rat's version of what a boy is. Tess had no desire to have a name-image anything like that.

'You, huh?' said Long Nose again.

Tess said nothing.

'Huh? Huh?'

When she still made no reply, he gave her a

command that no rat will ever refuse, because too often their lives depend upon it.

'Freeze!'

Tess froze. But Long Nose did not. He walked all around her from her nose to her tail, muttering to himself. 'Huh? Huh? Nananana. Nope. Huh?' He tugged at her tail and her whiskers, prodded her nose and looked into her ears. He lifted her feet and counted her teeth and made her sit up on her tail while he examined her belly, all the while saying: 'Huh? Nope. Nanana. Nope.' At last he went round behind her and started fiddling with her tail again.

'Tail two toes short, huh?' he said.

Tess didn't catch the image. 'Huh?' she said.

'Three toes, four toes, huh?'

'Huh?' She turned around to see what he was doing, just as he bit off the last inch and a half of her tail.

Tess squeaked and swung round ready to attack, but Long Nose looked amazed and offered his throat in defence.

'Hurt!' she said. 'Tail, yowch!'

'Seven toes,' said Long Nose, holding up the end of her tail and measuring it against his front paw. 'You, Tail Short Seven Toes.'

Tess examined the wound on her tail and was surprised to see that it was hardly bleeding at all. Nor was it anywhere near as sore as she had expected. She could live with it, she decided, and would almost have forgiven Long Nose had she not turned round to find him contentedly eating the end of her tail for his breakfast. She shot him an insult that even he could not fail to understand, and ran ahead to find Kevin.

The rats feasted on the rubbish in the basement of the restaurant. There were other rats there, too, pleased to meet the newcomers and exchange the latest gossip. One of them, a handsome fellow who introduced himself to Tess as Stuck Six Days in a Gutter Pipe, showed her how to recognise rat poison and scatter bits of it around to make it look as if it had been eaten. Then he helped her to find the choicest bits of leftover food, such as fish spines, chicken hearts and slivers of soap. Tess accepted them as graciously as her rat nature permitted, but it seemed to her with her great hunger that anything she ate was as good as the next thing, and that was even better.

There was plenty for everyone and the place seemed to have a constant turnover of rodent customers who came and went in a leisurely fashion. Stuck Six Days in a Gutter Pipe wrinkled his nose suavely at Tess as he left, but the effect was slightly spoiled by the chicken leg in his mouth that he was taking home for the children.

When Tess had eaten all she could, she joined Kevin and One Black Whisker in a quiet corner where they were chatting with two unknown rats.

'Guides,' Kevin told her. 'Long Nose, One Black Whisker curled up asleep in the couch on the waste ground. Little old woman sitting beside a fire, many streets. Long Nose and One Black Whisker confused, lost.'

'Many street, huh?' said Tess. 'Boy, girl walking, riding on a bus. Owls, pigeons flying. Us rats going slowly. Us rats very tired. Us rats sleeping.'

'Boy, girl scratching their heads,' said Kevin. 'Looking at maps, shrugging their shoulders.'

'Us rats swimming in sewers, us rats in slimy black drainpipes.'

'Girl going into her house, huh?' Kevin's black eyes were cold and mistrustful and Tess knew her own must have looked the same. But he was right. There was no turning back now, and no way of knowing where to go without the guidance of the city rats. She showed Kevin her teeth for spite, but a few minutes later they were back on the rat highways with their new guides.

CHAPTER NINE

For three more nights Tess and Kevin travelled through the rats' city underground, changing guides twice more along the way. They ate from rubbish bins knocked over by dogs, from shop store-rooms and from the shelves of poorly guarded kitchens. When they reached the outskirts of the city they began to travel above the ground, and they stopped many times along the way in urban gardens to feed on fresh vegetables and tasty scraps from compost heaps. Rats, it seemed, were never short of food.

On the fourth day, dawn found them in one of the most affluent areas of the country. Green fields and trees surrounded impressive houses, both old and new, owned by those people who could afford the luxury of having the best of both worlds. Tess was aware that her parents had checked out areas like this before they settled on the house beside the park. The air was so fresh and the country smells so sweet that she found herself regretting their choice. What was puzzling her, though, was that the sort of area they were in didn't fit at all with the picture the rats had given her of the little old lady who was waiting beside the fire.

'Little old lady, huh?' she said to their latest guide. Her name was Nose Broken by a Mousetrap, and it was easy to see why.

'Yep, yep, little old lady,' she said, and darted through a hedge into a field of lush grass.

It was not snowing now, but there had been several light snowfalls over the last few days, and because of the relentless cold, whatever snow had settled had remained. It stuck to the rats now as they dislodged it from the grass, and melted in dark patches on their glossy coats. They stayed close in to the hedge to avoid the eyes of dogs or hawks or passers-by, and soon they crossed into a second meadow, and then a third. A road ran parallel to their route, between the meadows and the widely spaced houses on the opposite side, and the occasional car passed along it, driving slowly because of the icy conditions. After a while, Tess realised by the change in sound that the hedge they were following was no longer beside the road but running away from it and out into the open country.

'Road, huh?' she said. 'Little old lady house, huh?'

'Yep, yep,' said Nose Broken by a Mousetrap, and she led the way through the twisted roots of the hedge. They stopped on the other side. They were on the edge of a green track with high brambly hedges on each side. Blackthorn and ash trees grew overhead so as to make it almost a tunnel. It was a track for people and animals only, far too narrow for a car.

'House,' said Nose Broken by a Mousetrap, twitching her nose along the path.

'House, huh?' said Kevin.

'House, yep. Little old lady. Yep, yep. Careful. Cats. Many cats. Follow soak-away pipe. Passage through hollow walls, comes out above the fireplace. Cats can't reach.' She touched noses with each of them and said: 'Nose Broken by a Mousetrap visiting her grandchildren. No hair yet. Many streets.' And with that she was gone, back through the hedge and out of their lives.

'House,' said Kevin, and started running down the track. But this time Tess didn't follow.

'Freeze!' she said.

He did, instantly. Tess looked up and down the track. She sniffed the air and listened carefully for a while. They were well hidden from the road by a bend in the track, and the hedges were high on either side. With a sigh of relief, she Switched into human form, and after a moment or two, Kevin did the same.

Tess hollowed her back, stretched her arms above her head, and then swung them around like a windmill, all those things that a rat can't do. Then she sighed again and sat down against the base of a tree where the ground was free from snow.

'Shove up,' said Kevin.

Tess moved over, turning away from him, and he squeezed in beside her with his back against hers. 'What did you do that for?' he said.

'Do what?'

'Change.'

'We're going to see a little old lady, aren't we?'

'Yes. But she obviously speaks Rat, doesn't she? How else could she have sent the others looking for us, huh?'

'Don't "huh?" me,' snapped Tess. 'I'm fed up with being a rat. That wasn't part of the deal as far as I'm concerned. It's all right for you. You're used to it. Maybe too used to it.'

'Oh,' said Kevin, 'like that, is it? Well, maybe you're too used to being a rotten human. We didn't make the stinking sewers and slimy drainpipes, you know? You did. We don't leave rubbish thrown around all over the place. It's your lot who does that. You're lucky you've got us to clean up after you!'

Tess was staring at him, open-mouthed.

'What's wrong?' he said.

'What do you mean, "us"?'

Kevin looked at the ground and gathered a small lump of snow in his hand.

'What do you mean, Kevin?' Tess went on. 'What are you trying to say?'

'Nothing,' he said. 'It's just that I'm not good at being a boy. With rats you know where you stand even if it isn't always pleasant. But I don't understand people properly. They say one thing and they mean another. I don't know how to look at them and I don't understand the way they look at me.'

Tess looked around her. A weak morning sun was pouring yellow light through the branches and picking out specks of brilliance in the thin snow. Above their heads the birds were chatting quietly, not too concerned by their presence but aware of it all the same.

'I don't either, Kevin,' she said, gently. 'I'm not sure anybody does. That's just the way people are.'

'That's fair enough I suppose,' he said. 'But it doesn't give me a good reason to bother with them.'

'You keep saying "them", or "you", as if you don't

belong. But you do. You're the same as any of us when it comes down to it.'

'Am I, Tess?'

'Of course you are! We're all the same underneath.'

Kevin sighed deeply and tilted back his head so that it rested, just for an instant, against hers.

They walked together down the path until the house came into view. It was a tiny place and quite ancient, completely at odds with the surrounding wealth and grandeur. A few hens picked at the grass around the front door, and a troop of ducks that were puddling around in the mud beside an outside tap took offence at the presence of strangers and waddled away in a line, quacking contemptuously.

The little old lady heard them and came to the door.

'At last,' she said. 'I thought you'd never get here, so I did.'

'Pardon?' said Tess.

'I been waiting ages,' said the little old lady. 'You took your time, didn't you?' She threw a suspicious glance at Kevin and said: 'I thought you was a rat.'

'Huh?' thought Kevin instinctively. He looked crestfallen and hung behind Tess as they followed the old woman into the house.

'Never mind,' she said, pushing cats off chairs beside the fire to make room for them to sit down. 'I suppose you is a rat and you isn't. It's all the same in the end. All the same to me at any rate. Sit yourselves down, and don't take any notice of them cats. A knee is a knee to a cat and a lap is a lap, and whether it's a knee or a lap it's warmer than the floor. If you doesn't like cats,' she looked pointedly at Kevin, 'you can tell them where to get off, but politely, mind, because we doesn't tolerate rudeness in this house, does we, pussums, eh?'

She closed the hall door behind them and they settled, a little self-consciously, into the newly vacated chairs. The fire was crackling brightly, and a large black kettle on a hook above it was wheezing in a way that made Tess hopeful of tea. It seemed like a year since she had tasted it.

The cats didn't turn out to be a problem because as soon as the old woman sat down they began to gather on her lap, and before long there were four of them there, manoeuvring for position.

'Tell us your names,' said the old woman. 'Come on, don't be shy. No rules in this house except that you minds your manners and doesn't be anything nasty to scare the cats. And you needn't think you're so special, either, sitting there like that. We was all young once, you know. You isn't the only ones who was able to Switch yourselves.'

'We know that,' said Tess.

'You knows everything, that's your trouble. Teenagers always does. There's nothing anyone can tell them. Teenagers is arrogant, that's what they is. Isn't that true, pussums, eh?'

The four cats had settled comfortably now and sat gazing out at Tess and Kevin with narrow, malevolent eyes. Kevin was looking pointedly at the floor, and Tess knew that he wasn't going to be any help at all.

'Well,' she said. 'He's Kevin and I'm Tess.'

'Oh,' said the old woman. 'Kevin, is he? That's a good, solid name, now, Kevin is. You can't argue with that, can you?'

'I suppose not,' said Tess.

'But Tess,' the old woman went on, without pausing for breath, 'isn't a name at all. It's one of

75

those ridiculous new inventions like a sticky label. They might as well have given you a number, miss, as a name like that.'

'But that's not true!' said Tess, beginning to get annoyed. 'It's a very old name.'

'A very old name? How can it be a very old name when you's only a little nipper, eh? I'll tell you a very old name. Lizzie is a very old name, and I isn't telling you how old it is, and as every young gentleman knows,' she leant forward and poked Kevin on the knee so that he jumped, 'it isn't polite to ask. But you can take it from me, it's a very old name. It's very nearly about as old a name as you can get.'

There was an awkward silence, during which the kettle's voice moved up a semitone. Tess glanced around the room, surreptitiously. Beside the fireplace was an old black oven, and above it Tess noticed a hole in the stonework of the chimney front which she recognised from Nose Broken by a Mousetrap's description. She could well imagine Lizzie sitting there in the evenings, having conversations with little twitching noses poking out, while the cats prowled below in impotent fury.

Behind them was a small table, and beyond that an old-fashioned square sink between cupboards with broken doors. There was a litter of bits and pieces everywhere, but Tess had the impression that, on the whole, the place was clean. Light streamed in from a large window behind the sink. Tess took a second look, unable to trust what she had seen. Hanging on a line above the window, like an eccentric pelmet, were a half dozen pairs of Lizzie's drawers.

Tess tried not to laugh. She looked at Kevin, but

he was rubbing imaginary dirt off the palm of his hand, and she realised that he was inwardly fuming.

'Is Lizzie your name, then?' she said, still battling with the giggles that were threatening to erupt.

'It isn't what I'd have chosen if I was given the choice,' said the old woman, 'but we never is, is we? There it is, as soon as we's big enough to know it, and then we's stuck with it, isn't we? We can't shake it off, can we pussums, eh? Born Lizzie I was, and Lizzie I'll be to the end of my days if there ever is an end to them.'

Tess realised that Kevin was swearing silently, in Rat.

'You has a very lazy tongue, young man,' said Lizzie, 'but a nasty, busy little mind. And you's very stupid if you thinks I can't know what you's saying.'

Kevin looked up, shocked. 'Sorry,' he said. 'I forgot.'

'You forgot, so you did. Teenagers always forgets. Teenagers thinks they's the only ones with eyes and the only ones with brains. I was a rat, young Kevin, before your father had an eye to have a gleam in. I was a rat in the days when those things wasn't done, and many other things besides. I was a rat in days when teenagers wasn't allowed. What do you think of that, eh?'

Kevin looked daggers at Tess and she glared back at him. It hadn't been her idea to come here. It was becoming clear to her that the old woman was mad as a hatter. Her parents would be at home, out of their minds with worry, and she had spent four nights in the sewers of Dublin to come and listen to total nonsense.

Lizzie put the cats down off her knee, one by one,

and got up. She reached out and gave the kettle a prod so that it swayed on its hook and hissed angrily.

'Get a move on,' she said to it. 'You's always slow when I's in a hurry. You does it on purpose.'

The hissing died down and a few weak puffs of steam escaped from the spout. 'These days,' Lizzie went on, 'anything goes, doesn't it, eh pussums? Anyone who wants to can be a teenager. You sees them everywhere with their hair all painted and their raggedy clothes and every one of them knows better than the next one. Oh, it's an awful thing. Dreadful. It's catching, too. It's an epidemic. And some people is never cured, never. Some people is teenagers all their lives. Isn't that right, pussums?'

Kevin stood up and turned to Tess. 'I've had enough of this,' he said.

'Oh?' said Lizzie, putting her hands on her hips. 'Had enough, has you? You hasn't had anything yet, so how is it you's had enough? If you's had enough, why did you come at all?'

'Come on, Tess,' said Kevin. Tess stood up a little uncertainly, looking from one to the other.

'That's teenagers for you,' Lizzie went on, her voice rising in tone to near hysteria. 'They hasn't even started and they's had enough. They only wants to sit in front of the TV or have a good time for theirselves being jackdaws and puppies and toads. They hasn't time to sit and chat. They always has to go. They's always had enough, even before they's had what they come for!'

Kevin wheeled on her, and the cats, which had occupied her vacated chair, scattered in all directions. 'And what about stupid old women? Who invites . . . who invite people to visit them and drag them right across Dublin and then tell them to mind their manners so they can stand there and abuse them?'

'You hasn't any manners to mind!' shouted Lizzie.

'Listen who's talking!' yelled Kevin, and he stormed out. Tess made to follow him, but in the dim hallway of the little cottage she hesitated and stopped. She could hear the old woman muttering to her cats, and she crept back and stood beside the hall door, where she could hear but couldn't be seen.

'They's all the same, Tibsy,' Lizzie was saying. 'They's all the same, isn't they, Moppet?'

Tess heard the springs of Lizzie's chair creak as she sank into it. 'But we's done it again, hasn't we? I's done it again. You gets offended sometimes, doesn't you? But you forgets. Them people never forgets. They didn't even let us tell them about the krools, did they? They was in too much of a hurry to get offended and be gone.' Her voice went quiet and Tess suspected that she was close to tears. 'Now what's we going to do?'

Kevin was halfway up the little path before Tess caught up with him. She was very relieved that he hadn't Switched, because she would have had a lot of difficulty finding a rat, and as for a pigeon or a hawk, it would have been hopeless. The fact that he hadn't changed meant that there was still a chance.

'Wait, Kevin,' she said.

'What for?'

'I want to talk to you for a minute.'

'Talk?' he said. 'That's all people ever do. Talk, talk, talk. They talk so much they get on each others' nerves and what happens then? They have to bloody well talk about it!'

'Don't be like that, Kevin.'

'Why not? What's the point of all that talking, eh?

Now you want to talk about that stupid old woman, and we wouldn't be here in the first place if it wasn't for her talking too much.'

'Will you just listen for a minute?'

Kevin sighed and turned to face her. His eyes were grim and determined, and her heart sank. He could disappear so easily, just vanish from her life into the skies or the underground passages of the city and she would never be able to find him again.

'Don't you see?' she said. 'The old woman is like you. She doesn't understand people either. She doesn't know how to behave.'

Kevin looked away from her. 'It just proves my point, doesn't it?' he said. 'It's a waste of time trying to understand people.' But Tess knew that he was disarmed now.

'All right, then,' she said, and then, in Rat: 'Girl going into her house. Rat crawling into the hollow couch.'

Kevin looked at her again, and she could see that his anger was dissolving.

'Maybe it will all turn out to be a wild goose chase,' she said, 'but we can't just give up without finding out. We have to hear what she has to say.'

'It's one thing hearing what she has to say and another thing understanding it! Where does she get that accent from, anyway?'

'I don't know. She's not from around here, that's for sure. Maybe she's from England somewhere?'

'More like Mars, I'd say. But if you want to hear more of it, go ahead. I'll wait here.'

'No. You come with me. Come on. She's sorry now.'

'And so she should be.'

Tess looked back towards the house. 'Do you know something, Kevin?' she said.

'What?'

'You care a lot more about people that you think you do.'

'Oh, do I?' His voice was full of contempt. 'Why do you think that?'

'Because if you really didn't care, if you really thought people were so useless, then they couldn't upset you, could they? Because you'd never expect anything better.'

Kevin didn't answer, but looked at Tess suspiciously. She began to walk back down the path towards the house and after a while he followed.

CHAPTER TEN

At that moment, in the sealed and bug-proofed room in the Pentagon, there was another meeting going on. Many of the same faces were there, but there were one or two changes. Colonel Dunkelburger was absent. And the newly elected President of the USA, Mr Dan Doyle, was there at the head of the table.

The meeting had been in progress for some time and the two tapes had been played by General Snow, and then played again.

'Maybe those guys in the snowmobile just woke up a polar bear or something?' said President Doyle.

No one ventured to answer. In the light of what they had just heard, the question seemed to answer itself. After a while, the President said: 'Well, what are we supposed to think? That there's some kind of aliens up there or something?'

Again no one answered. Quite a few of those

present had already come to the unpleasant conclusion that there was no other explanation.

'Hey,' the President went on, 'all kinds of things happen to guys when they're out in the snow too long. They get snow blind. They get cabin fever, that kind of thing. Hell, my great grand-uncle Zacchariah was holed up in the mountains for sixteen weeks once with nothing but a pair of wolverines for company. He was never the same again.'

General Wolfe cleared his throat. 'Er, that's quite understandable, Mr President.'

'Sure is,' said Doyle, brightly.

'But, the thing is, I guess maybe this isn't quite the same kind of situation.'

'No, I'm sure it isn't. But from what I can see, we got nothing at all to go on except a hell of a lot of snow. These things happen sometimes, you know? Two years ago we had a drought that went on a bit too long, and suddenly everybody was saying that the end of the world was nigh. People were saying the Russians were behind it, and maybe they were. But we didn't panic. We didn't go off bang and start losing our heads about it. I don't know about the rest of you guys, but I reckon that if the USA can win one Cold War, we can win another.' He slapped his knee and laughed aloud. One or two of the others tried their best to join him, but failed.

General Wolfe cleared his throat again. 'That's very good, sir,' he said, 'and there's no doubt at all that we all have to take that kind of attitude to this, uh, little problem we have out here . . .'

'Frankly, sir,' said General Snow, glancing disdainfully at Wolfe, 'we feel that this problem may be a bit more serious than that.'

'You think the Russians are involved?'

'No, sir. We have no reason to suspect that. In fact, from what we can make out, they're having a much worse time of it than we are. What I'd like to bring to your attention, if I may, is that these weather conditions are like nothing that's been seen on earth in recorded history. The satellites are sending us pretty uncanny pictures. Those storms are radiating outwards from the polar circle in something approaching perfect symmetry, and it's kind of hard to believe that whatever is causing that is a natural phenomenon.'

'Well, that may be,' said President Doyle, 'but I find it harder to believe that it's an unnatural one. I just can't go for these alien theories, gentlemen. I'm sorry.'

'That's OK, sir,' said General Snow. 'No one expects you to. But whatever we all of us personally suspect or believe, we need to decide on what kind of action we're going to take.'

There was a silence, while everyone followed their own thoughts, and then the President said: 'Maybe it's the FCOs.'

'FCOs, sir?' said Dunwoody.

'Yeah. You know. The gas they use in those little spray cans? Pfft. Pfft. Deodorants, that kind of thing. Maybe we should ban them. Would that help, maybe?'

'Er . . . that's CFOs, sir,' said Dunwoody, 'and we already banned them.'

'With all due respect, sir,' said General Wolfe, 'I think we have to be prepared to go a little further than stamping out deodorants to get to the heart of this mess.'

'Right. OK. I see you guys mean business. I like that. That's the true American spirit. So, what do you want to do? Do you want to throw a few nukes in there to be on the safe side? It's OK by me if you do. It'd be good for public morale. Show that we're doing something. Show the rest of the world that America cares.'

'It's . . . that's a very good idea, Mr President,' said General Snow, 'but I think it might be a bit risky.'

'Risky? Why? There's nobody up there, is there?'

'Not as far as we know. But the effects of atomic radiation can be a little unpredictable, as you know. The winds can blow it around the place and into inhabited regions. And besides that, there's the little problem that nuclear weapons aren't too popular with the public right now.'

'OK. Nukes are out, then. How about . . . let's see now . . . how about saturation bombing?'

General Wolfe's jaw dropped. 'Saturation bombing of the whole Polar region?'

'Too big, huh?'

'Way too big, sir.'

'Well, how about starting in the middle and work your way outwards? See what happens?'

'It's a little beyond our resources, sir,' said General Wolfe. 'And as a matter of fact, while we're on the subject of resources – '

'You looking for a raise? You got it. I like your attitude to this problem.'

'Thank-you, sir,' said Wolfe. 'Would you mind making a note of that, Mr Dunwoody? But what I was coming round to saying was that General Snow and I have been having some discussions. We feel that in order to get a better understanding of the Arctic situation we're going to need to get more satellites up there. We also need to get more planes in the air to overfly the area with radar, and we need some pretty damn fast research into anti-stealth detection equipment. We need more planes up above those storms and more planes down in the middle of them, taking pictures with radar and infra-red and every other thing we got at our disposal. We can't fight this enemy until we find out what it is, sir, and for that we need a bigger budget.'

'Ah,' said the President. 'Well, you know money is kind of tight right now. You're all aware we've got an increasing number of refug – er, visitors from Canada and Alaska staying with us for a while, and it's looking like there's going to be a bit of a crisis on the home front if this weather keeps up.'

'That's just my point, sir,' said Wolfe. 'We need funds to do whatever is necessary to avert that crisis.'

'Oh, yeah. I see. Well, I guess you guys had better produce some figures.'

General Snow nodded, and Wolfe opened his briefcase.

Lizzie was delighted to see Tess and Kevin back, though she did her best to hide it.

'Here they are again, pussums,' she said. 'You just never knows, does you. Forgot your tea, did you? Never mind, kettle's nearly boiling.' She poked it again and it swayed and spat water on to the fire where the drops fizzed and steamed.

'Find your chairs, find your chairs, they's still there, no cats back in them yet. Plenty of chairs, the cats hasn't worn them all out yet, make yourselves comfortable while I makes the tea. Come in, Oedipus, before you gets shut out.' She closed the hall door firmly behind a black tomcat and leant on it for an instant, smiling at Tess and Kevin as brightly as she could manage. Then she fell into such a frenzy of activity that it made Tess nervous just to look at her.

'Where's the milk, eh? Has you had it, Moppet? No, no, that's yesterday's milk. Where did I put it now, I wonder? Well, there's not many places it can be. Oops, kettle's boiling, let's just get these tea leaves out into the garden. Does you know that, Tessie?'

'What?'

'Tea leaves is good for the garden. Nothing better. Straight out the window on to the grass they goes and the hens scratches them in. Nothing better. I never puts no manure on that grass out there and there's no greener grass in the country.'

There was nothing Tess hated more than being called Tessie, but she bit her tongue and said nothing.

'Warm up the teapot, now,' Lizzie went on. 'Have to warm the teapot, does you know that, eh? Does you warm the teapot? Takes all the good out of the tea if the teapot isn't warm. I never gets a decent cup of tea anywhere except in my own house. All these teenagers, see? They never does anything properly. They hasn't any patience. Not yourselves, of course, yourselves is different. Yourselves has good manners. See how you sits there so quiet and not rude at all. Mind you, I's still sure they told me you was a rat. Hard to know the difference sometimes. Specially these days. Things was different when I was young. We was moving around, see, always on the go, we was. Here today, gone tomorrow. But the one thing we brought with us wherever we went was our manners.'

Kevin was looking steadfastly down at the floor between his feet.

'Not that we was gypsies, mind,' said Lizzie. 'We never had anything to do with that sort.' She paused

87

for a moment and looked around, as though not quite sure where she was. Then her pale blue eyes brightened. 'I suppose that milk is still out in the pantry. Of course it is. It's cooling down, that's what it's doing. Don't go away now, little Switchers. I'll be back in a second.'

Tess nudged Kevin's shoulder. He looked up sternly, then dropped his guard and smiled. Lizzie came back and bumbled around in cupboards for a while, collecting an assortment of chipped cups and odd saucers. At last, after what seemed an age, she handed them each a piping hot cup of tea and sat down in her chair with her own.

Tess took a sip of her tea. It was hideously sweet, but what bothered her more than that was the hair in it that stuck to her tongue. She picked it out as politely as she could. It was short and white and rather thick. Lizzie's hair was white, too, but it was long and silky and tied in a tight french knot at the back of her head. There was no way this hair belonged to her.

Kevin seemed to approve of the tea. He sat back in his chair and sipped it slowly. 'Very good,' he said to Lizzie.

'Ah!' she said. 'You speaks then? I wasn't sure. I wasn't sure at all.'

It was the worst thing she could have said in the circumstances. Kevin scowled and retreated back into sullen silence.

Tess risked another sip of her tea. It tasted better now that the hair was gone, but there was still something about it that was slightly off-putting. 'I suppose we'd better get down to business,' she said.

'Business?' said Lizzie. 'What business? I can't stand business. Never has anything to do with it. All them fields out there is mine, you know, and there's a track worn to my door with business people coming to try and buy them off me. What does they want with them, says I? I never seen a farmer in a suit like they wears.' She laughed suddenly, long and loud. 'I tells them to take their business back where they came from and keep it out of my fields.'

'But they must be worth a fortune!' said Kevin. 'Why don't you sell them?'

'What does I want with a fortune?' said Lizzie. 'I has a fortune already. I has a house of my own and my cats and hens and ducks and my Nancy. I has green fields all around me and I likes it that way. I lets the farmer use the land and he brings me everything I needs from the shops. What's that if it isn't a fortune?'

'But you could live anywhere. Have anything you want.'

'I lives somewhere already, and I has everything I wants. I did enough travelling for a dozen lifetimes before I married and came here. What would I want to be taking to the roads for at this time of my life?'

For a moment all three of them were silent, and then Lizzie looked at Kevin and said: 'Now I knows you isn't a rat.'

Kevin clicked his tongue and sighed in exasperation. Tess sniffed the tea and had a nasty suspicion that she knew who Nancy was, but she decided to ignore it and think of more important things. 'I didn't really mean that kind of business,' she said. 'I meant the business of why we're here. Why you told the rats to bring us here.'

'Oh,' said Lizzie. 'That's something different altogether, isn't it? That's not business. That's a matter of altogether more urgency, that is.'

'Right,' said Tess, gently. 'Then perhaps it'd be a good idea if we talked about it.'

'Oh, not now,' said Lizzie. 'No, that would never do.'

'But you just said it was urgent,' said Kevin.

'There's some things in life,' said Lizzie, 'that just can't be talked about when the sun is shining and the birds are singing. There's some things that aren't fit to be seen, or heard, or said, or even thought in the daytime, no matter how urgent they is.' She threw Kevin a disdainful glance. 'If you was a rat, you'd know that.'

Kevin got to his feet in exasperation and stuffed his hands into the pockets of his jeans. 'Then I'm going out for a walk,' he said.

'Hold on,' said Lizzie. 'We'll all go in a few minutes, and you can meet Nancy. But let's have another cup of tea first. After all, it isn't every day I has a couple of young Switchers to visit me.'

CHAPTER ELEVEN

When Tess and Kevin had finished their second cup of tea, Lizzie brought them out to the back of the cottage to meet Nancy. She was a white goat, as Tess had suspected, and she was tethered by a long rope in a scrubby field which lay between the orchard and the ruins of what was once a large and rather grand house.

'I lived there once,' said Lizzie, 'many years ago. But it was too big for me all on my own. I prefers the cottage.'

Nancy stayed where she was as the three of them approached, and chewed her cud with weary patience as Lizzie prattled over her. Tess had something of the same distaste for goats that she had for rats. They were the poor relations of the other farmyard animals, always bony, always hungry, always eating what they shouldn't.

'There now, Nancy,' Lizzie was saying. 'Isn't you

a lovely goat? You's the best little goat in the world, so you is. You's my poppet. This here is Kevin, and this one is Tessie. They's Switchers, both of them. You can believe me or not believe me, it makes no difference to me, but they is. Don't you wish you was a Switcher, Nancy? I bet you does.'

Nancy spotted a few green bramble leaves that she had missed earlier in the day and barged her way between her admirers to go and collect them. Lizzie looked a bit embarrassed. 'She's very fond of me, really,' she said. 'But she's shy of strangers. Was you ever a goat?'

Kevin nodded, but Tess shook her head.

'Really, Tess?' said Kevin. 'Were you never?'

'No.'

'But why not?'

'Oh, I don't know. I never fancied it, I suppose.'

'Goats is all right,' said Lizzie, 'except that they has poor manners. Not Nancy, of course. Nancy has manners.'

But Nancy wasn't there to display them. She had disappeared around the other side of a clump of brambles and was straining as hard as she could on her tether.

'They has brains, though,' Lizzie went on. 'Goats has wonderful brains. Ten times as many as sheep has.'

'It's true, Tess,' said Kevin. 'Why don't you try it, eh? We could go for a spin.'

'You can't do that,' said Lizzie. 'That's bad manners. You's only just arrived.'

'But we wouldn't be long, would we Tess? Just a quick spin.' He turned a little further towards her so that Lizzie couldn't see his face, then he widened his eyes in a pleading way, and Tess realised that she was being very slow. He just wanted an excuse to get away from the old woman for a while.

'Oh,' she said, 'all right. I suppose it could be interesting.'

'Now I thinks about it,' said Lizzie, 'it's not such a bad idea. You two could do me a favour.'

'How?' said Kevin, slightly suspicious.

'Easy. There's a few gardens around here that could do with a bit of a trim by a pair of goats. They's an awful toffee-nosed crowd, those ones up the road. They sneers at me if I's out for a stroll. They thinks they's better than me what with all their fancy cars and posh clothes and their business and all. The way they talks! Pfoo! You can smell it.'

Kevin looked at Tess with mischief shining in his eyes. 'Come on. What are you waiting for?'

Tess hesitated, thinking of her own mother and her love for her garden, wherever she found herself. And her father had a fancy car and good suits and worked in what Lizzie scornfully referred to as 'business'. If they had bought a house here instead of near the park, it might have been her own garden they were intending to 'trim'. She looked at Kevin. He was waiting eagerly for her reply. They were living on opposite sides of the tracks, she realised. And yet, they were alike.

'You thinks about things too much, young lady,' said Lizzie.

'That's true,' said Kevin. 'She's right for once.'

'You bad-mannered little pup!' said Lizzie. 'Go on, the two of you. Get out of here and eat some shrubs while you still has the chance.'

Kevin winked at Tess and looked around. They were well hidden, there among the bushes and trees.

'Make sure you isn't white, now, whatever else

you does,' said Lizzie. 'I don't want anyone coming blaming my Nancy.'

Tess was converted. While Lizzie watched, they made their change. Nancy stared around the edge of the bushes, astonished by the sudden appearance of two goats, one brown and one black.

'Ooh,' said Lizzie. 'That did me the power of good, that did. Makes me feel young again.'

But none of the three goats understood a word that she said.

Tess and Kevin hopped over the stone wall which bounded the scrubby field and into a small orchard. Behind them they could hear Nancy bleating pathetically at the loss of her new friends. For a moment or two they dithered, drawn quite strongly by the call of one of their own kind, but then they moved off among the trees.

Tess knew immediately why the others had been so keen that she try out being a goat. She had been sheep, cattle, horses, and recently she had quite often been a deer along with the others in the Phoenix Park, but none of them had felt quite like this. She had realised quite some time ago that her ability to experience the lives and beings of other creatures had an effect upon her personality as a human being. Each time she changed, something of what she learnt of the animal character stayed with her. She had developed quickness of reaction and awareness of her surroundings from the timid creatures of the fields and woodlands: the mice and squirrels and birds. From the farmyard animals she had learnt patience and a kind of resignation. Now, as she felt the full-blooded mischievous nature of the goat, its sharpness and its love of life and wildness and freedom, she became aware of how tame and careful her life had always been. The values that she had absorbed in her succession of comfortable homes and high-class schools had prejudiced her more deeply than she supposed. She had always avoided those animals which had characteristics that she perceived belonged to people of a different, inferior class. She had never experienced life as nature's scoundrels because of her fear of their human counterparts. Foxes, bats, crows and magpies, rats and stoats were all villainous creatures in her imagination. She had seen herself as being on the other side of an ongoing battle between good and evil.

Now things were beginning to change. Some of that change was certainly brought about by the days and nights of existence as a rat, when she had experienced for herself how it felt to live outside the law, despised and hunted. But there had been good things about it, too. She had discovered a new sense of courage, and a willingness to stand up and put that courage to the test when she had to. It had been exhilarating. She remembered how she had felt when Long Nose had bitten off her tail. She had been utterly fearless at that moment. It had been a very different feeling from her prim and petty resistance of Kevin when they had first met, and she suspected that she would have more useful resources to draw on now if a similar occasion arose. Her time as a rat, and even more so this new, exciting exploration of goatness, had given her a new understanding of Kevin. He was the kind of boy that she knew her parents would view with contempt. They would mistrust his guarded and suspicious manner and be shocked by his outbursts of temper and foul language. He could not, by any stretch of the imagination be classified as 'our kind of person'. But

Tess had been into his world now, and experienced it from the inside. She knew how all those alien and conflicting feelings arose in him, and how he could not live the life he did without them.

As Tess mused, she and Kevin were wandering slowly through the orchard and browsing on the leaves and twigs that fell within their reach. There were windfalls lying on the ground, apples and pears, but they were small and hard and bitter because of the long spell of cold. The leaves had suffered too, and those that had not already fallen were fibrous and dry, but to a goat they were as delicious as mature cheese.

Tess was surprised by some of the things that she was learning. She found that it was a myth that goats would eat anything. On the contrary, her senses of smell and taste were so refined that she could tell in an instant whether a moth had laid eggs on a leaf or a bird dropping had landed there, even a month ago. She would leave anything that was the slightest bit tainted where it was on the tree, and eat carefully around it. She found that she had a rich and rare sense of her own independence, and that, much as she enjoyed the pleasure of Kevin's company, she would depart from him without hesitation if the need arose. Nancy was still bleating on the other side of the hedge, and although Tess recognised that the sound held within it the desire for company, she knew that Nancy was calling for more than that. For stronger than every other emotion in a goat's heart is the love of freedom. Even here, amid the luxury of the rich lands where food would never be scarce, her goat soul longed for the high, craggy places of the world, places which are of no use to mankind but are the wild, windy kingdoms of the goats.

She and Kevin browsed their way peacefully to the edge of the orchard where two strands of barbed wire reinforced a neglected hedge. On the other side of it, cattle were grazing.

Kevin turned to Tess, and the sly, mischievous glint was in his eye again. Tess knew that for the first time, she was returning it. Together they slipped through the fence as if it wasn't there and strolled out into the field.

The cattle stared, disconcerted, and swung to face them, blowing blasts of steaming air from their nostrils. For the hell of it, Kevin jumped at them, and they spun on their heels with surprising speed and careered away across the field. A goat can't laugh, but Tess's heart stretched with mirth as she watched them. Stupid creatures. She despised them.

From where she and Kevin stood, they could see the neatly trimmed hedges of the nearest house, and with another quick glance of agreement, they set out towards it. Behind them the cattle recovered themselves and followed cautiously, closely grouped for safety.

The garden they had seen proved to be impenetrable. The cattle were held back by barbed wire which prevented them from getting anywhere near the hedge, but this was no deterrent to the goats. Nor was the hedge itself, for it was immature and full of gaps. It was fortified, however, by a heavy chain-link fence that even a goat could not work loose, and the two sides of the property that had no hedge were guarded by a high stone wall. Tess and Kevin spent a while nibbling at the protruding sprigs of the hedge, but there was no damage they could do, so they left it and stepped out into the road.

A goat can see over great distances and hear sounds

from miles away if it chooses to do so. In the normal course of events, however, it doesn't waste its attention in this way, but holds it to a much smaller radius around its immediate environment. It was not greatly surprising to either Tess or Kevin, therefore, when they found themselves stepping right into the path of an oncoming car. Nor was it particularly dangerous, because a goat thinks fast and acts faster. They sprang out of the way, feeling nothing more than a brief moment of excitement which made them jump and dance for a few yards along the verge, just for the joy of existence. The driver, however, got the fright of her life when the two shaggy goats appeared from nowhere, and she swerved much more violently than was necessary to avoid them. When she eventually calmed herself down and reversed out of the hedge, there was a hole in it that would have taken the two goats a week to eat.

Lizzie was standing with Nancy in the scrub behind her house.

'Hush, now, Nancy,' she was saying. 'Shhh. Don't you worry about them two.' She peered between the trees. 'Where is they, anyway? They's gone out of sight, Nancy. They's disappeared.'

As it happened, they had disappeared from Nancy's mind at around the same moment, leaving an abrupt vacuum which she filled by lying down in calm detachment and chewing her cud.

'There's no sign of them at all, Nancy,' said Lizzie. 'I suppose they's forgotten us.' She was right.

The next house the two goats met was surrounded by a stone wall with a wide coping stone running along the top. The wall was high enough to deter a stray cow or sheep, and more than high enough to contain the little terrier who yapped at them from the other side of the gates. He was one of those pampered little dogs that are somehow never to be found in farmyards or houses that have children, and he had never in his life encountered a boot or a rough hand. To protect him against the cold, he wore a red tartan jacket which made him feel a lot bigger and stronger than he ought to have done.

Kevin hopped effortlessly up on to the top of the wall, and Tess joined him. The little dog began to yap hysterically, halfway between the garden wall and the safety of the house, halfway between rage and terror. Inside the house, his mistress turned up the volume on the TV to cover the noise he was making. He hadn't been outside for long, and the fresh air was good for him.

Kevin jumped down without warning and ran full tilt at the dog, who paused for an instant in astonishment, then ran yelping around the side of the house. When Kevin gave up the chase and returned to nibble the top off a young Japanese willow, the terrier took up a position on the corner of the house and stood there, watching, with his tail between his legs.

The hours passed. Lizzie pottered around the house and garden and waited for her visitors to return. Around mid-afternoon she hacked a couple of parsnips out of the frozen ground of her garden, and collected carrots and a turnip from the potting shed where they were stored in boxes of sand.

'They shouldn't be hungry by the time they gets back,' she said to Nancy, 'but in my experience them teenagers always is, no matter how much you gives them.'

She brought the vegetables into the kitchen and

ran water into the sink. Outside the window the sky
had clouded over, and as she stood there wondering
if it was going to start snowing, she saw a policeman
coming down the path.

'Watch out, pussums,' she said. 'You'd better make
yourselves scarce. Here comes trouble.'

CHAPTER TWELVE

Lizzie went out into the little hallway of her house and stood beside the hat-stand. The policeman knocked on the door. Lizzie sat perfectly still and waited. Moppet offered to sit on her knee, but Lizzie shook her head and held up a hand to stop her. The policeman knocked again. Lizzie reached out and rocked the hat-stand gently, so that it made mysterious creaking and rattling sounds. Then she waited again. After a while, the policeman knocked a third time and called out: 'Hello?'

Lizzie stood up and opened the kitchen door and closed it. Then she did it again.

'Hello?' called the policeman. 'Anybody home?'

Lizzie went into the kitchen and over to the window, where she made a big show of peering round the folds of the curtain. The policeman saw her, smiled, and lifted his cap.

'Who is it?' said Lizzie.

'No need to be afraid,' said the policeman. 'I'd just like a word with you for a minute.'

'What about?'

'Can I come in? It's awful cold out here.'

Lizzie went back out into the hallway, where she rocked the hat-stand again, tidied up a pile of newspapers and re-arranged the coats on their pegs. There was another knock.

'All right!' said Lizzie, impatiently. 'I's coming.'

At last she opened the door. The policeman made as if to come inside, but Lizzie stood solidly in the doorway and didn't move. He sighed. 'Garda John Maloney,' he said. 'I believe you're known as Lizzie?'

'That's right, yes.'

'Are you by any chance missing two goats?'

'Goats?' said Lizzie. 'I hasn't got two goats, so how could I be missing them?'

'I see. Your neighbours led us to believe that you kept goats.'

'I has one goat. Just one. Her name is Nancy and she's tied up out in the brambles where she always is. Who told you I keeps goats? If anyone has any complaints about Nancy they can bring them to me theirselves or else keep their mouths shut. Nancy has better manners than the rest of that lot put together.'

'No, no,' said the Garda. 'It's nothing like that. It's just that we've got rather a problem, you see.'

And they had, too. In a more built-up area, there might have been some chance of driving those two goats into a corner, but out there in the leafy suburbs, they hadn't a chance.

Tess and Kevin, communicating by a combination of goat gestures and Rat images, were having a ball. Three members of the Garda Siochana and a gathering of neighbourhood residents were red in the face with exertion and fury, but remained utterly helpless. The goats dodged and scrambled, jumped walls and pushed through hedges. They split up without hesitation when they had to, and met up again as soon as they could, and they avoided traps with uncanny and infuriating ease. A local farmer had been called in to help and he had arrived full of cool confidence with his two best sheep dogs. But ten minutes after he arrived, the farmer was coaxing the terrified creatures back into his Land Rover and wondering if they would ever have the courage to work again. Few dogs are a match for a full-grown goat, and a dog that has worked all its life with timid, flock-minded sheep is particularly helpless when it finds itself suddenly looking into the unflinching yellow eyes of one of their brazen cousins.

Lizzie's policeman rejoined the others, leaving her to carry on making her stew. It was simmering away nicely when she heard the two goats returning, their hooves clattering on the frozen ground as they came careering down her path. They swung at full speed into the yard at the side of the house and veered in through the open door of the woodshed. A few seconds later, Tess and Kevin emerged laughing, their eyes still shining with mischief. They had barely got inside the door of the house when three men came running down the path. They stopped outside the front door, blowing hard. One of them was the Garda who had visited Lizzie earlier in the day. The other two were local residents. Lizzie knew one of them, a short heavily-built man wearing a tweed jacket and white breeches. He was a banker, and he had tried on more than one occasion to get her to part with her land.

She got up from her chair and threw open the window. 'Clear off!' she said. 'We got no goats in here. We doesn't want you coming galumphing in here and frightening our chickens and our Nancy. Clear off.'

'But we know they're around here now, Ma'm,' said Garda Maloney. 'We followed them down your track.'

'Well they isn't here now, and we wants to have our dinner in peace. So clear off.'

Garda Maloney restrained his rising temper with some difficulty. 'I'm sorry, Ma'm,' he said, 'but those two goats have been causing havoc up on the estate up there.'

'Neighbourhood, Garda, if you don't mind,' said the banker. 'It's not an estate.'

Maloney sighed in exasperation. 'Neighbourhood,' he said. 'They've been causing havoc in the neighbourhood and I must insist that we have a look round.'

'Have you got a search warrant?' asked Lizzie and, before there was time for an answer, she shut the window and turned her back on it.

'Come on, Lizzie,' said Tess. 'Why don't you let them look? They won't find anything.'

'I don't want them poking around in my sheds and my garden, that's why. And I wants to have my dinner.'

'We'll show them around, then, me and Kevin. We'll make sure they don't go poking around. OK, Kevin?'

'Not me,' said Kevin. 'I don't like peelers. You show them around if you like.'

'Right then, I will.'

Tess went out and opened the front door to the three men. They had started out towards the yard, intending to have a look around whatever Lizzie might say. Tess joined them. 'I'll show you around the place,' she said.

Garda Maloney smiled pleasantly and said: 'Very good of you,' but he looked at her just a little too long, and all at once, Tess's blood ran cold. What a fool she was. What a complete and utter fool. Of course her parents would have told the police that she was missing, no matter what she had said in her note to them. She turned away and tried to collect her thoughts. 'Where do you want to look first?' she said.

'Everywhere,' said the banker. 'We'll start in here.' He looked into the woodshed, and the other neighbourhood resident, who was tall and thin and dressed in a ridiculous one-piece down ski-suit, peered in over his shoulder. Garda Maloney, however, seemed more interested in Tess. 'Are you a relative of the old bird, then?' he asked.

'She's not an old bird,' said Tess, thinking like a rat, thinking like a goat, wishing that she hadn't been so snobbish and knew what it was to think like a fox. 'She's my Aunt Lizzie. My great-aunt, actually.'

'Ah,' said Maloney.

Tess led the way purposefully towards the hen-house. Lizzie had been around feeding shortly before, and the hens were still gathered around the trough, pecking at the last crumbs of their mash.

The policeman watched them, absently. 'Just down for the day, are you?'

'Yes. My father will be here later to pick us up.'

'I see. You and your brother, is it?'

'Yes.'

He nodded, casually. He wasn't sure where it was he'd seen her face, or even whether he had seen it at all, but there was something about her that was ringing a bell. He could check it out later, when he got back to the station, but in the meantime it was important that he didn't raise her suspicions and drive her off.

'Nice part of the country, isn't it?' he said.

'Not particularly,' said Tess. 'I'd prefer to go to the sea if I had the choice.'

She led them on around the back. Nancy had been milked and put to bed in her own corner of the cowshed. 'If there were any more goats around,' said Tess, 'she'd be going ape. They don't like being on their own, goats don't. But you can look around in the field if you want to. And the orchard's through there.'

'Like animals, do you?' said Maloney.

'Not particularly. But Aunt Lizzie does. She never stops talking about them. There's nothing she doesn't know about animals. And,' she added, conspiratorially, 'nothing she doesn't tell you. Whether you want to know or not.'

Garda Maloney was beginning to think that he was mistaken. This girl was far too relaxed to be on the run. He smiled at her and she shrugged and lifted her eyes to heaven. 'Family duty,' she said.

The other two were just closing the door of the potting shed. 'Nothing there,' said the sporty one.

'No,' said Garda Maloney. 'I think we'd better call it off. With any luck they're on their way back to wherever they came from. If they do turn up again you can let us know, and we'll have another try in the morning.'

'You'll have to get your marksmen with tranquillizer darts,' said Tess.

Maloney laughed. 'Yes, we'll certainly need

someone like that. Let's hope that's the end of them, though.' He followed her back to the front of the house and started with the others back up the track. 'Give my regards to your aunt,' he said. Tess looked heavenwards again and ducked in through the doorway.

Kevin and Lizzie were sitting in the fireside chairs. Lizzie was eating stew out of a jelly mould and Kevin was eating his out of a small, dented saucepan with a bent handle.

'We left the dish for you,' said Lizzie, pointing to the hob beside the fire.

'Never mind that,' said Tess, looking daggers at Kevin. 'That was a great bit of thinking, that was, Mr Rat, Mr Street-wise, Mr Hedgehog-brain!' Kevin stared at her in amazement as she went on: 'And you have the nerve to tell me that I'm all right, Jack!'

'What are you talking about?'

'I'm talking about you, looking after Number One. You don't like peelers, oh, no. What about me, then?'

'Children!' said Lizzie. 'Stop squabbling! Where's your manners?'

'Oh, shut up about manners, Lizzie,' snapped Tess. 'And we're not children. This has nothing to do with you. I'm talking to this selfish little swine.'

Kevin was growing darker by the minute, like a heavy cloud, waiting to burst. 'I don't know what she's talking about,' he said.

'I'm talking about the Gardai! I'm talking about missing persons, descriptions, photographs. I'm talking about being on their records!'

Kevin swore. Lizzie looked as if she might object, but changed her mind.

'You should have thought of that, Kevin,' said Tess. 'You should have warned me.'

'It isn't my fault! It was your idea. "Oh, la di da, come on, Kevin, let's show the nice gentlemen around." I didn't want to have anything to do with it!'

'But I don't think like you do. I wasn't brought up like that. It's your job to think of things like that!'

'And who do you think you are? Telling me what my job is!' He glared at her with such contempt that her anger evaporated and left a dull ache in the pit of her stomach.

'Come on, now, girls and boys,' said Lizzie. 'Stop arguing and eat your dinner while it's hot.'

Kevin poked around lethargically with his spoon. 'Did he recognise you?' he asked, sulkily.

'I'm not sure. I think he did, but I might have put him off the scent.'

'Not to worry,' said Lizzie. 'No sense in getting edgy, is there?' She handed Tess her stew in the dish they had saved for her. Tess looked at it gloomily. It had DOG written on the side.

CHAPTER THIRTEEN

Lizzie refused to let Tess and Kevin help her wash up, even though they really meant it when they offered. So they sat beside the fire and watched the flames licking round the kettle as she clattered around behind them.

'Funny thing,' said Tess, emerging from her own thoughts, 'but I can still feel the place where Long Nose bit off my tail. Ridiculous, isn't it, when I haven't even got a tail.'

'Like a phantom limb, I suppose,' said Kevin. 'You were lucky it was only your tail, though. If it had been your hand or your nose or something you'd be in a bit of a mess now, wouldn't you?'

'What do you mean?'

'Didn't you realise that? If you get injured it doesn't just go away, you know.'

Tess did know. She had often noticed that scratches and bruises from her animal exploits stayed with her when she Switched back to herself. But it had never occurred to her that something more serious might happen.

Kevin was unlacing his shoe. 'You probably didn't notice but I only have three toes on this foot. I got the other two stuck in a crack in a drain pipe once, and there was no way to get out except to just keep pulling.'

'Yeucch!' said Tess.

Kevin took off his sock. It was dark and stiff with dirt, and Tess was about to pass a comment on it when she saw his foot, and forgot about it. The last two toes, the smallest ones, were missing. It was slightly grotesque. 'Doesn't matter what I am,' he said. 'If it has toes, those two are missing.'

Tess thought about what he had said, about how it would be if she had lost a hand, or even a whole arm or leg. Kevin had started rubbing at the dirt between his remaining toes. 'Put it away, will you?' she said. 'It's disgusting.'

He shrugged and pulled his sock back on. Behind them, Lizzie closed a cupboard door with an emphatic bang.

Tess leaned back in her chair and closed her eyes. She was suddenly very tired. Up until now it had all been a kind of a dream for her. While she was a rat, it had been difficult to think about human matters, and then there had been the meeting with Lizzie and the reckless, capricious delight of their goat afternoon. But the episode with the policeman, and now Kevin's foot, had brought her back to earth. All through her childhood her strange ability had been something that was private and carefully contained. It was safe, that other world, and it had always been tidily separate from her 'real' life. But suddenly, over the last few days, it seemed to have moved beyond her control. She was no longer at all certain of who she was and what she was doing. Kevin was elusive and confusing. At times she was so sure that she had at last found the companion that she had been looking for all her life, and then something would shift and he seemed to be at odds with her, almost an enemy.

And then there was Lizzie. What was anyone to make of Lizzie? It had all seemed to make some kind of sense when they set out, as though there was a mission for them, but in the light of police searches and sleepless parents pacing the floor at home it seemed like madness. She didn't know what was real and what was not. She was suddenly, horribly afraid that they might all be mad.

'Tess?' said Kevin.

'Yes?'

He was looking at her carefully, and his concern was evident in his face. Here was yet another Kevin, one that she hadn't seen before now. But how did she know if she could trust him?

'Are you all right?' he said.

'I just don't really know what's going on.'

'I feel like that sometimes, too. But you know there's nothing to keep you here, don't you? You can go home right now if you want to.'

Tess looked across at Lizzie. She was drying the last of the cutlery with a grimy tea-towel, and Tess noticed that she was doing it rather quietly and thoughtfully, listening to their conversation. Her face was different, somehow, as though she were no longer trying to keep a distance between herself and the youngsters. The games were over. All three of them were ready, it seemed, to be serious.

'Maybe we should just hear what Lizzie has to say,' said Kevin, 'and then we can decide what to do. What do you say?'

Tess relaxed. She nodded and sighed, and settled more comfortably into her chair. As if in approval of her decision, a tabby cat hopped lightly up beside her and curled itself up on her lap.

Back at the Garda barracks, John Maloney carried his dinner tray over to a free table in the cafeteria. It was more usual for him to go home when his shift was over, because he preferred to cook for himself and was quite good at it. But today he was too exhausted to even think about it. His mind was littered with images of goats which did improbable things, and he couldn't shut them out, no matter what he did. He sat down and began to eat, but he couldn't taste the food. However hard he tried, he found he couldn't be concerned about whatever public menace those goats were causing. There were far more serious matters in police duty. But what irritated him was the feeling of having been defeated by a pair of dumb beasts.

Out of the corner of his eye, John spotted Garda Griffin leaving the check-out with his tray. He looked away quickly, but he knew he had been seen and that Griffin was coming to join him. Now he was in for a ragging. Oliver Griffin was one of those people who can never take anything seriously in life, or at least, pretend that they can't. John had worked with him for a while in a different part of town, and they had spent many a night on patrol together. In a crisis, Oliver was about the finest person he had ever worked with, because nothing, not even the most tense of situations, could deprive him of his sense of the ridiculous. There were times when John had found knots in his stomach being dissolved by unexpected laughter. But in the normal run of things, Oliver's eternal quipping was intolerable.

'Tough day, eh?' he said now, as he unloaded his tray. This was his breakfast. He had just arrived for the night shift. 'Job getting your goat?'

'Don't start, Olly,' said John. 'I'm not in the mood.'

'Ah, come on. It can't be that bad. Bit of sport for a change. Headline news. Big game hunting in Tibradden, County Dublin.'

'I wouldn't care if I never saw another goat in my life. If you'd had to deal with them you wouldn't be laughing.'

'Want to bet?'

John laughed despite himself and felt a lot better. 'The worst of it was,' he said, 'the little sods seemed to be enjoying themselves. You'd swear they were taking the mickey out of us.'

'Probably were,' said Griffin. 'And I hear you had an encounter with the Lady of the Manor.'

'Who?'

'Old Lizzie.'

'Oh, her. Do you know her, then? Some character, eh?'

'Yes. Sitting on a fortune and still living like a gypsy.'

'A fortune? What makes you think that?'

'All that land. All those fields around there. They all belong to her. About eighty acres, I think. Imagine what that's worth.'

'Phew!' said John.

Oliver finished his pudding and went on to his main course. John had seen it enough times now not to be surprised, but it still made him feel slightly queasy. 'Yes,' Oliver said. 'The developers are hovering round her like flies, but she won't sell. "I has all I needs," ' he mimicked, ' "and I needs all I has." '

The accuracy of the imitation had John laughing again. 'You must have been trying to buy the place yourself.'

'Na. I've known Lizzie for years. She's a great old character, really. There's more to her than meets the eye. I often stop in there for a cup of tea when no one's looking.'

'Naughty, naughty.'

'Public relations, John, public relations. And she's lonely out there on her own. Where's the harm in it?'

'I suppose so.' John put down his knife and fork and started peeling an orange, trying not to look at the red puddles of ketchup on his friend's plate.

'Besides,' Oliver went on, 'I feel sorry for her in a way, with half of Dublin's biggest speculators waiting around for her to die. Imagine thinking that the only thing the world wants from you is your death, eh? And like I said, she's not bad company once you get to know her. She still tells me to clear off whenever she sees me, but if you ignore her she gets quite friendly sometimes.'

'Hardly my idea of fun,' said John.

'Ah, don't be so cynical.' Oliver paused to slurp at his mug of tea, then went on: 'You can't get fun out of life unless you give it a chance, you know. I'll be sorry when Lizzie does snuff it, but I'll get a great laugh out of it, too. Can you imagine the faces of those Ballsbridge dudes when they find out she's left the lot to a home for retired donkeys?'

'Donkeys?'

'Well, she probably will, you know. Or goats. That'd be a good one. I wonder what the "Neighbourhood Residential Committee" would think of that?'

John smiled, despite himself. 'She couldn't do that, though,' he said. 'Her relatives would be entitled to collect, wouldn't they?'

'What relatives? Lizzie hasn't got any relatives.'

'Yes she has. I met her niece today, or her great-niece or something.'

Oliver was shaking his head with a certainty that infuriated John. 'Nope,' he said. 'Not Lizzie's, you didn't. She told me herself that she has no one left in England and she never had a family of her own here. "I's all alone in the world and I likes it that way. I's no time at all for people, I hasn't. They takes up too much space." '

'Well, you're wrong this time, Olly. I – ' He stopped abruptly. The gentle tapping of suspicion that he'd had when he first saw Tess had become a mighty hammering. 'Drink your tea, Olly,' he said as he stood up.

'Why? Where are you going?'

'We're going, Olly. Missing Persons.'

'I knowed it was going to happen,' said Lizzie. 'I knowed it as soon as I read about it in the newspaper.'

Kevin looked across at Tess and raised a quizzical eyebrow. Tess shrugged.

'I doesn't get newspapers to read,' Lizzie went on. 'I hasn't any interest in all them politics and wars all over the place. I gets the papers from Mr Quigley. That's the farmer who owns those cattle. He gives me his old ones to light the fire. I hasn't any time for fire-lighters. They smells like motor cars.'

Tess stroked the cat on her lap. She was relaxed now that she was sure she would soon be home. She didn't know what she was going to say to her parents, but she would think about that later.

'Sometimes I looks at them before I scrunches them up,' said Lizzie, 'and sometimes I doesn't. I always knows that if something's important it'll catch my eye. How can something be important if you has to go looking for it, that's what I says. So I wasn't surprised when I saw it.'

'Saw what?' said Kevin.

'About that drilling up there in the North Pole. I knew what would happen if they started all that carry-on. But people never thinks about what might happen. They wants oil and they wants money and cars and fire-lighters, and as soon as they's got them what does they do but want more of them? So I said to myself, I'll warn them. That's what I'll do.'

She got up a little stiffly and went over to the kitchen sink. The night had fallen, so she drew the curtains, and for a while the room was soft with firelight. Lizzie rummaged around in a drawer until she found what she was looking for, then turned on the light and came back to her seat.

'There,' she said, handing a piece of brown paper to Kevin. 'That's only a copy, mind. I always keeps a copy of letters. Not that I ever writes any these days. The real one was on good paper. The best you can buy, Mr Quigley said.'

Tess leant across and read the letter over Kevin's shoulder. At the top it said, 'To The Taoiseach And the Tanaiste of The Dail, KilDare Street, Dublin. From Mrs Elizabeth Larkin of TiBradden, Co. Dublin, OWNER of Much Land and VaLuable ProPerty.

'They has to know that you's someone,' said Lizzie,

proudly, 'before they takes any notice of you. They doesn't pay no attention to commoners.'

Tess and Kevin read on. The writing was large and untidy, with small letters and capitals all jumbled up together.

> 'YoU Cant alloW ThoSe comPanY PeoPle to Go driLLing UP in the NorTh PoLe. OR elSe YoU WiLL LeT ouT The krooLs and Then YoU WiLL Be SoRRY.
> YoURS finaLLY,
> Lizzie Larkin.
> PS PLeaSe Send a coPY to The comPanY ThaT iS doing The dRiLLing becauSe I don'T have There adReSS.

Tess sat back in her chair. She knew without doubt where that letter would have ended its life, and she wondered how many similar letters from cranks passed through government offices in the course of a year. She sighed and sat back. The cat made a tour of her lap and resettled itself.

'Well?' said Lizzie. 'What does you think?'

'It's a good letter, Lizzie,' said Tess. 'It's very good. But the trouble is, people don't . . . I mean people in government don't very often take much notice of letters.'

'Whoever they're from,' Kevin added.

'You's right, there,' said Lizzie, 'and you knows why that is, doesn't you?'

'Why?'

'Because they thinks they knows it all, that's why.'

Tess's face was among the first that John Maloney saw in the room where the files on missing persons were kept. 'There she is,' he said to Oliver Griffin. 'I knew I'd seen her before.'

'Who?'

'Lizzie's niece.'

'But Lizzie hasn't got a niece,' said Oliver.

'I believe you, Olly,' said John. 'Now let's go.'

'People in general,' said Lizzie, 'thinks they knows it all. And if they doesn't know it then they puts it in front of a microscope or a periscope and makes it bigger, and there's things in this world should be left the same size they always was and not interfered with at all.'

Tess looked at her watch. She would be home before her parents went to bed.

'They doesn't use plain common sense,' Lizzie went on. 'They sees things that is plain and simple and they goes to great lengths to make them as difficult and complicated as they can. They sees that the world is cold at both ends so they comes up with a cock and bull story about how we's all spinning around in the air like a football. But you can throw a football around all day and it never gets colder at the ends than it is in the middle.'

'I don't think it's the spinning that causes the Poles to be cold, Lizzie,' said Kevin. 'I think it's the way the earth tilts.'

'Tilts?'

'Yes. It's sort of leaning as it goes around, so some bits don't get as much sun.'

'And where did you find that out?'

'I read about it in the library.'

Lizzie got up angrily, spilling two cats on to the floor. 'That's exactly what I's talking about,' she said. 'What does a nice boy like you want to go poking around libraries for? Nosing out all kinds of nonsense you has no use for? Then when you gets a chance of learning what you needs to know, there's no room left in your head for it.' She strode over to the fire. 'And you get a move on!' she said to the kettle, giving it a poke.

'Why don't you tell us anyway, Lizzie?' said Tess. 'About your krools.'

'My krools?' said Lizzie. 'They isn't *my* krools. They isn't anybody's krools. They's just krools.'

'Well, tell us about them anyway, will you?'

'We's too far south to know about them here, that's all. They knows about them in Finland and Norwieg-erland, and they knows about them in Siberia, except they has a different name for them. They's big, cold, flat things like jellyfishes, and they sleeps in their own ice just like the grizzly bear sleeps in his own fat. They sleeps for thousands and thousands of years and while they's sleeping they doesn't bother the rest of the world. But if they gets woken up they gets hungry, and off they goes across the world, filling theirselves up again.'

Tess glanced at Kevin, hoping to share a silent joke, but he was gazing solemnly into the fire.

'What about the other cold places, Lizzie?' he said. 'Like the Alps and the Himalayas.'

'Those mountains, you mean? But they's cold because they's high up in the sky! Everyone knows that!'

There was a long silence. Tess moved her chair a bit closer to the fire. Outside the wind was getting up and she could hear the cat-flap on the outside door rattling. At last, Lizzie sighed and shook her head sadly. 'You doesn't believe me,' she said. 'I was afraid you wouldn't.'

The others said nothing, because there was nothing they could say. From time to time, the wind made the chimney give a great pull which sucked flames up to hug the kettle.

'You doesn't believe in krools,' said Lizzie, 'and I suppose you doesn't believe in them dinosaurs, either.'

'But dinosaurs are different,' said Tess. 'There's evidence for the dinosaurs. You can still see their bones.'

'We doesn't know what it was left them bones behind,' said Lizzie, 'and krools has no bones to leave, in any case. But if those dinosaurs was there, where are they now?'

Kevin was becoming irritable. 'Everyone knows that, Lizzie. They became extinct.'

'And does everyone know what happened to make them extinct?'

'There was a shift in the earth's crust and something changed in the atmosphere. That's what happened.'

'There was earthquakes,' said Lizzie, 'and they woke up the krools, that's what happened. And the krools was hungry when they woke up, that's what happened. And the krools ate up all the dinosaurs that wasn't already dead and buried. That, young clever clogs, is what happened.'

Tess felt a shiver run up her spine. It was the kind of shiver she sometimes got when she read a good poem or heard a piece of music that touched on some deep and delicate truth that everyday language didn't reach. There was another long silence, and then Lizzie said: 'It's snowing. I can smell it.'

The two policemen parked their car some distance

from the top of Lizzie's track. Before they got out, they emptied all the loose change from their pockets and put it in the glove compartment. Oliver took the car key off its ring and left the others under the seat. There must be nothing that would clink or jangle. They intended their approach to be silent.

Lizzie's kettle was starting to sing. This time she knew where the milk was and she had already emptied the teapot but even so there was plenty for her to bustle with. 'Switchers isn't what they used to be,' she said. 'There was things we knew in those days that you doesn't even begin to know.'

'But what could we do, Lizzie?' said Tess. 'Even if we did . . . I mean, even if it was true about the krools?'

'It is true,' said Lizzie.

'Even if it is,' Tess repeated. 'What could me and Kevin do about it?'

Lizzie thought for a moment, swirling hot water around the teapot. 'I doesn't know exactly,' she said. 'I's been thinking about it a lot, and I doesn't know exactly. But I know this. Switchers has powers that you hasn't even dreamed about. You hasn't even begun to know what you can do.'

'What do you mean?' said Kevin, suddenly interested.

Lizzie emptied the hot water into the sink. 'I knows all the things you two has been. I can see it. You could see it, too, if you was watching properly. And I knows that you hasn't done half the things I did when I was your age. You hasn't a notion of how much you can do.'

'What can we do, Lizzie?'

'Even I doesn't know that. But now it's too late I

wishes I had my time all over again. We all thinks we has all the time in the world when we's young. And sometimes we doesn't push ourselves hard enough. We doesn't use our imagination, so we never really gets to the bottom of ourselves. Sometimes we doesn't know what we could be until it's too late.'

Kevin was listening intently, but Tess's mind was beginning to wander. Lizzie sounded too much like her parents and her teachers, sounding off about how young people didn't make the most of themselves. She looked at her watch again. She would have time for tea, she decided, and while she was drinking it she could try and work out a way to get Kevin on his own and arrange another meeting. She didn't want to go home without being sure that she was going to see him again.

Lizzie poured water on to the tea leaves.

And then the knock came at the door.

CHAPTER FOURTEEN

'Lizzie?' called Oliver from the front door. 'Don't worry. It's only me, Garda Griffin.' He knocked again, without waiting. 'But don't waste my time now, you hear? Open up the door.'

'All right, all right,' said Lizzie, making her way through the hall. 'I's coming.' She turned on the outside light, opened the door, and peered shrewishly at Oliver. 'What does you want at this hour? Scaring old ladies in the middle of the night! You ought to be ashamed of yourself.'

Oliver stepped past her into the hall and went ahead of her into the kitchen.

'Sorry, Lizzie,' he said. 'But it's official business this time.' He was both relieved and disappointed to find that there was no sign of any young runaways.

'Well, I don't understand it,' said Lizzie, following him into the room and closing the door behind them. 'I never in my life heard so much fuss about a pair of goats. And look at you! You should have knocked those boots on the step before you came in. You's dragging snow all over my floor.'

'Sorry about that,' said Oliver. 'But this time it's not about goats. It's those two youngsters we're looking for. The ones who were here earlier on.'

'Why? What's they done?'

'Can I get through this way, Lizzie? To the back?'

'What you want to go out there for? There's nothing out there.'

Oliver went through the scullery and into the back porch, where he opened the door for John.

'What's he doing there?' asked Lizzie. 'What's going on? Why can't he use the front door like everyone else?'

'We're just being careful,' said Oliver. 'In case anyone slipped out the back.'

'Who's going to slip out the back? What's you talking about?'

'I don't think they're here,' said Oliver to John. 'But you'd better take a look upstairs, just in case.'

'No, he hadn't,' said Lizzie indignantly. 'And don't you talk above my head as if I wasn't there! I's smaller than you is, but I's older than the two of you put together and you has no right to barge into my house as if you owned the place.'

Oliver sighed. 'I'm sorry, Lizzie. You're right. We're just a bit worked up because we had trouble with your path in the dark. One of your trees has confiscated John's cap and won't give it back.'

'I'll have a word with it in the morning,' said Lizzie.

'It's all right. I'm sure we'll find it on the way back. We didn't use our torches on the way down because we didn't want anyone to see us coming.'

'You was sneaking up on us, wasn't you?'

'Who's us?' said John, casually.

'Me and Nancy and the pussums,' said Lizzie. 'They was sneaking up on us, pussums, so they was. Looking for that nice young boy and girl who was here. What's they done, anyway?'

'We don't think they've done anything very wrong, Lizzie, but the young girl has run away from home and her parents are very worried about her.'

'Oh, dear,' said Lizzie. 'And I thought they was such a nice pair of youngsters. Is you sure it was her?'

'Positive,' said John.

'Then they told me a pack of lies. I always says you can never trust them teenagers.'

'How long have they been gone?' said Oliver.

'Let me see, now. They left just after this young man was here looking for the goats, I think.'

'But maybe you're expecting them back?' said John.

'No. Why should I?'

'Well, I was just wondering why you have three cups set out on the table.'

There they were, three odd cups and three odd saucers with a jug of milk and a bowl of sugar beside them.

'Three cups,' said Lizzie. 'They's observant, isn't they, pussums, eh? Still, I suppose they has to be. That's what they's trained for. But maybe they's too clever, eh? Maybe there's things about an old woman's life that they didn't ought to ask?'

John felt a slight chill and looked around the room. The little old house was creepy enough at night, even with the lights on. He hadn't enjoyed the dark walk down the lane one bit.

'We have to ask, I'm afraid, Lizzie,' said Oliver. 'That's our job.'

'They has to ask, pussums. But maybe they'd prefer if they didn't know?' She went over to the table and poured a drop of milk into each of the three cups. 'I does this every night before I goes to bed. And in the morning, when I gets up, I does it again.' She poured the tea and spooned in sugar. Then she put one of the cups in front of her and one to each side. 'This one's for me,' she said, 'and this one's for my husband George, who went off over the sea to fight in the war and never came home. And this one here is for our little daughter Kitty who died before she was even born.'

John shuffled his feet in embarrassment. The cottage had suddenly become saturated by the most appalling sense of loneliness. Even Oliver was silent.

'So,' said Lizzie, brightly. 'Up you goes and take a look around upstairs. Go on with you.'

'That's all right, Lizzie,' said Oliver. 'It won't be necessary.'

'Indeed it will. You has a job to do and you's required to do it. And I has a reputation to protect. I won't let anyone have cause for doubt in case they says, "Maybe she was hiding those two young criminals all along." Go on. Up you goes.'

'They're not criminals, Lizzie,' said Oliver.

'Never mind.' She bustled them out towards the hallway. 'The bulb is blown in the hall but there's a switch at the top of the stairs. Go on.'

The two policemen obeyed, sheepishly, and thumped up the narrow stairs. They stayed there only long enough to poke their heads around the doors of the two small bedrooms, then they came down again.

'Sorry about all this, Lizzie,' said Oliver. 'We didn't mean to disturb you.'

'You's more disturbed than I is, by the looks of

things,' said Lizzie. 'Why don't you sit yourselves down and drink these cups of tea now they're poured?'

John blanched, and even Oliver's cast-iron stomach became momentarily queasy. 'It's very kind of you,' he said, 'but I think we should move on.' He reached down and picked up a ginger tomcat who had been asleep in Lizzie's chair. 'I see you have a new cat?'

'I has two new cats,' said Lizzie. 'So you needn't be minding about me and my little habits. I has all the company I needs.'

Oliver put the cat down and led the way to the front door. 'Did they say where they were going when they left?'

'They said they was going home. "Time we was going home," that's all.'

Oliver retied his scarf and pulled his coat tight around him. 'That's where Garda Maloney's going, too. Wish I was. Goodnight, Lizzie.'

'Goodnight.'

The two men lit their flashlamps and were soon hidden from sight by the blizzard. Lizzie closed the door and went back to the kitchen, passing on her way the army parka and down jacket that were hanging among her coats in the hall. 'That was a close shave, pussums,' she said. But she got no response, not even a glance. Every one of the six cats in the room was sound asleep. Lizzie looked at the three cups on the table. For a moment the loneliness still lying in the air closed in and settled on her heart.

Tess woke shortly before dawn. The fire had died down during the night and the room had become chilly. She yawned, then stood up and stretched, reaching out as far as her paws would go and catching them on the upholstery of the chair to check that her claws were sharp.

The other cats had gone on an inspection of the night and not yet returned. Someone was sitting in a chair pulled up close to the fireplace and Tess slipped down on to the floor with a view to finding a lap and getting warm enough to sleep again. But halfway there her other mind woke up, and she realised that it was Kevin.

She Switched, feeling rather glad that she hadn't made it as far as his knee before she realised. He jumped slightly as she appeared, then nodded briefly and returned his attention to the fire.

A few dry logs had been propped up in the embers, but they hadn't been there long enough to light. Kevin was leaning forward with his elbows on his knees, and it was clear that he was deep in thought. Tess pulled up another chair and spread her hands above the grate. 'Cold,' she said.

Kevin stirred and sighed but said nothing.

'I fell asleep,' said Tess. 'Cats are great, aren't they? There's nothing to beat a cat for comfort. I sometimes think that if I had to choose, I'd choose a cat.'

Still Kevin said nothing, but went on gazing into the fire. Tess looked at her watch. It was six-thirty. 'I meant to get home last night,' she said. 'But then I fell asleep. There's no point in going now because nobody'll be awake yet. Do you think Lizzie would mind if we made a cup of tea?'

Kevin threw her an icy look. 'Do what you want,' he said. 'Who cares?'

'You know what's wrong with you, don't you?' said Tess. 'You spent too long being a lizard. Personally I never found it much fun.'

Kevin's eyes blazed. 'And you spent too much time

being a flaming magpie, yakking away to yourself and getting on everybody's nerves.'

Tess swore in Rat, and Kevin swore back. The scores were level, and for a while they both stayed quiet. Small flames began to catch the base of the logs and creep up their sides. Behind them one of the cats came in through the scullery door, but went out again when she realised that neither of them was Lizzie.

At last, Kevin stood up and went over to the window. He pulled back the curtain and looked out into the darkness. Snowflakes were falling gently against the glass and little drifts had formed against the bottom of each pane. 'I don't mind if you go home, Tess,' he said. 'I won't blame you.'

'What do you mean?'

He let the curtain fall and came back to sit at the fire. 'I'd probably do the same thing if I were you,' he said.

'I don't understand,' said Tess. 'What else is there to do?'

'I'm going up there.'

'Up where?'

'To the Arctic.'

Tess stared, wide-eyed. 'What? To look for Lizzie's krools?'

'Why not?'

'Because . . . because it's crazy, Kevin, it's a laugh. You really believe they're up there? Giant slugs that cause ice ages?'

Kevin shrugged. 'I don't know.'

'Well, I do,' said Tess. 'Lizzie's not so bad when you get to know her, but she's not all there, you know. She's not the full shilling.'

'Is that right?'

'Of course it is. You saw that letter. She's harmless, but she's mad.'

'And what about us, Tess?'

'What about us?'

'Well, what would people call us if we told them what we do? What we are?'

'We don't tell them, though, do we?'

'Of course not. But why? What would they think if we did?'

Tess said nothing, not wanting to fall into the trap.

'Come on,' Kevin went on. 'What if you were to tell your parents where you've been for the last few days? What would they say?'

'They'd probably say I'd fallen in with a bad crowd and taken some funny drugs.'

'They might. But I'd say the chances are they'd take you to see a psychiatrist, wouldn't they? If you insisted on sticking to the truth.'

'Anyhow,' said Tess, 'that's different.'

'Why?'

'Because it is. Because we know the truth, and if the worst came to the worst we'd be able to prove it. But this business about krools is ridiculous.'

Kevin said nothing. The fire was burning brightly now and sending out sparks on to the hearth. Tess got up and filled the kettle at the sink. Outside in the trees, the first birds were beginning to complain about the weather. 'Besides,' she said, as she hung the kettle on its hook, 'even if it was true, which it isn't, what could we do? You and me?'

Kevin leant back in his chair. 'That's the whole point, Tess,' he said. 'That's why I'm going.'

'What do you mean?'

'Well, if you really want to know, I'm as doubtful about this krools business as you are. I wouldn't be going either, if it hadn't been for what Lizzie said about . . .' He paused.

'About what?'

'What was it that she said, exactly? Something about not knowing what we could do. Not knowing half of what we can do.'

'But we know that anyway, Kevin. Or I do, anyway. We're living in Ireland, you know? We can't go around the place being elephants and kangaroos and flamingos, can we? It'd be ridiculous.'

'I don't think that's what Lizzie was talking about.'

'What was she talking about, then?'

'I don't know. But when she said that, I had the strangest feeling all of a sudden. I can't really explain it, but it was as if I knew for certain that she was right, and that there was all this strength and power in me that I didn't know how to use. I felt like I was filled with it, just waiting to explode, except that I didn't know how to set it off. There was nowhere for it to go.'

Tess said nothing; not because she thought it was stupid, but because she was remembering times when she had felt like that herself.

'It's different for you,' Kevin went on. 'You still have a couple of years to play around with this thing, you know? Find out what you can do. But I don't. I don't have much time left at all.'

The kettle came to life with a long, low moan. Tess refrained from giving it a poke. 'I can understand that,' she said. 'But it still doesn't explain why you should want to go off on a wild goose chase up into the Arctic.'

'It does, though,' said Kevin. 'You remember the time when we were in the waste-ground and you didn't want to turn into a rat?'

'Yes.'

'Well, it's like that a lot of times in life, isn't it? Maybe you would never have taken that step if the dog hadn't come along and made you do it. But you did do it, didn't you? You could have flown away, but you didn't.'

'So what?' said Tess. 'To be quite honest with you, I'm not sure at this moment what good it did me.'

'Well, maybe it did and maybe it didn't,' said Kevin. 'And maybe not everything that happens ends up getting you what you want, or what you think you want. Maybe things happen for some other reason that we don't see straight away, or maybe they happen for no reason at all. You could spend your whole life worrying about why things turn out the way they do and you still wouldn't be able to fix it so that they always did you some good.'

'I didn't mean it like that,' said Tess, 'and you know I didn't.'

She gave in to her impulse to poke the kettle. It swung slowly backwards and forwards for a while, but instead of singing louder, it went silent again.

'I know you didn't,' said Kevin, 'and even if you did, it wouldn't matter. The thing is, I want to go. Everything in me wants to go, even though I know there probably aren't any krools.'

'But I don't think you're seeing things straight, Kevin. I mean, even if we . . . even if you did decide to go, how would you get there? All the animals are coming south, I've seen it on the news. The conditions up there are impossible for anything to live in.'

'But that's the whole point!' Kevin leant forward to look at her more directly, and his eyes were bright with excitement. 'Don't you see? Because sometimes we don't know what we can do until we have to do it. And if we always stick with what's easy and what's safe, then we'll never be made to find out. I'm not sure that I'd want to save the world, Tess, even if I thought there was anything to save it from, even if I could. But I want to know what I'm capable of, before it's too late.'

Tess heard Lizzie's footsteps on the stairs. Somehow the cats did, too, because they began to come in from outside, one at a time, shaking the snow from their paws.

'What's you two doing up so early?' said Lizzie.

'Just chatting,' said Kevin.

Lizzie put her hand on her hip and used it as a lever to straighten her back. 'Ooh. I's getting as stiff as a poker, so I is. All this cold weather doesn't do me any good. Hasn't they fed you yet, pussums? Hasn't they even given you a drop of milk? They's sitting there with all their important chatting to be done and you's all starving with the cold and with the hunger.'

The cats purred and wound themselves around her ankles. She poked the kettle, which dribbled on to the fire but began, a bit reluctantly, to sing. 'And has you come to any decisions with all that chat?' she went on. 'Is you going to go sledging or play snow-balls in the park?'

'I'm going north, Lizzie,' said Kevin.

Lizzie straightened up as though she were twenty-one again. 'I knew it,' she said to the cats. 'I told you, didn't I? He may not be all rat, I said, but he's got rat in him.'

Kevin laughed, and suddenly Tess felt remote from them, as though she had been excluded. She realised then for the first time that if Kevin went alone up to the North Pole, she might never see him again. It was possible that he would come back and look her up in her house in the park, but what if he didn't? And what if it kept on snowing, and they had to leave and go to Greece like the Sheehans? How would he find her then?

'And what about you, Tessie?' said Lizzie. 'What's you going to do?'

It hit Tess, then, with no warning, that expansive feeling which was so strong that it was hardly bearable. She was suddenly certain of her own strength and resourcefulness, and suddenly afraid of nothing.

'I, Lizzie,' she said, 'is going with him.'

CHAPTER FIFTEEN

Lizzie made pancakes for breakfast, which Tess and Kevin ate much faster than she could cook in the old black skillet. They drowned them in melted butter and golden syrup and ate them with their fingers, and nobody complained about the drips.

'Like Pancake Tuesday,' said Tess.

'Yes,' said Kevin, 'but let's hope we don't have to give up too much for Lent.'

Tess thought about the blizzards outside that they would be meeting for as long as they continued north. She still had no idea how they were going to travel, and her parents were trying to edge their way into her consciousness, threatening to destroy her resolve.

As though she were reading Tess's mind, Lizzie said: 'You thinks too much, girl. I's told you that before. And it's nothing but a waste of time. If you's finished with that pancake you better go over to the sink and wash your hands, because you isn't getting any more. I hasn't had one at all yet, and I's getting weak with the hunger watching you two stuff your faces.'

Tess got up and went over to the sink. Kevin followed. The water was icy cold and only hardened the butter on her fingers, but most of it came off on the towel. She handed it on to Kevin and looked out of the window. The snow had already made little ledges of itself on top of every level spot it could find. Every branch, twig and leaf bowed in submission beneath its weight. Tess could no longer remember the elated sense of power that she had felt before breakfast when she made the decision to go.

'Well? What's you waiting for?' said Lizzie. 'Off you go, get your coats on. There's no sense in standing around.'

Kevin went out into the hall and came back with their jackets. Tess put hers on, feeling like a small child who has been told to go out and play and has no choice in the matter. But it wasn't Lizzie, she knew, who was driving her to do it, or Kevin. It was her own pride. She was more afraid of letting herself down than of losing their respect.

'Lizzie,' said Kevin. 'There's something I want to ask you before we go.'

'Ask away,' said Lizzie, pouring batter into the pan.

'You know what you were saying about the power that we have? How we can do things we don't even know about?'

'Was I saying that? I suppose I was.'

'Well, can you tell us about it? So that we know what kind of things we can do?'

Lizzie shook the skillet so that the pancake slid around. 'I's been thinking about that,' she said, 'and I's decided that it isn't a good idea.'

'But why?' said Tess.

'Because I doesn't want to put ideas into your heads. Because if I puts ideas into your heads they might turn out to be the wrong ones. And there's nothing that gets in the way of a right idea more easily than a wrong one.'

'But can't you give us a clue, Lizzie?' said Kevin. 'A couple of examples?'

'That's just what I doesn't want to do. I has no idea what you's going to find along your way and I has no idea how you's going to deal with it. But I does know this. I'd lock that door this minute and holler as loud and as long as I could for Oliver Griffin and his ignorant pal if I thought you was going to be in any danger that you couldn't manage. I knows that I could do it if I was still a Switcher, and I knows without any doubt that you can do it, too. So get on your way before you starts thinking about things, and be sure to call in and see me as soon as you gets home.'

Kevin turned to Tess with a question in his eyes but she looked away and went towards the door. Her heart was numb with fear and she didn't want him to see it.

Lizzie came with them as far as the front step. 'Goodbye, now,' she said, as they walked out into the snow. 'Look after yourselves. And don't be too busy concerning yourselves with what is. There's times when it makes more sense to think about what isn't.'

Kevin turned to question her, but the door was closing in his face.

It was still early. Tess looked about her as they walked across Lizzie's front garden towards the narrow path. Apart from a few cat paw-prints, rapidly being filled in, there was not a mark on the snow. The birds were moving about in the trees and causing little avalanches among the branches, but they were not at all happy about the weather and saw no sense in going further afield before Lizzie came out to feed the chickens.

'What now?' said Tess.

Kevin shrugged. 'Fly, I suppose. There's no point in walking, is there?'

'Fly where?'

He shrugged again. 'North, I suppose.'

They moved closer together as they entered the narrow tunnel of the path.

'Just like that?' said Tess. 'Just fly north into a blizzard? Nothing worked out? No plans?'

'No plans,' said Kevin. 'No compass, no maps. And no hotels along the way, either, and no tents, no sleeping bags.' Abruptly he gave Tess a friendly shove so that she sidestepped into a shallow drift. His nose was red from the snowflakes blowing into his face, and he was grinning, so that Tess had the fleeting impression of a circus clown. 'We're leaving everything behind,' he said. 'We're on our own. No rules, not even Rat rules. Just the two of us, and all that out there.'

All that out there was still filling Tess's heart with dread, but Kevin's eyes were shining. 'Don't waste your fear, Tess. Save it up for when you need it, like the animals do.'

She smiled, despite herself, and he smiled back, more openly than he had ever done before. 'Pigeons?' he said.

Tess laughed, and they were friends beyond any shadow of a doubt, travelling with a common purpose. 'I hate pigeons,' she said. 'Why not be something bigger and faster? We can be anything we want. No one's going to see us in this snow.'

'Flamingos?'

'Eagles?'

'Swans?'

'Storks?'

'Albatrosses!'

'Yeah! Albatrosses.' And they were, squeezing awkwardly through the hedge, running with clumsy strides across the wide meadow beyond, and finally rising with slow, graceful wing-beats into the white heart of the blizzard.

Without thinking, without even wondering how they knew, they tilted their wings and were heading north. They flew high, to avoid the hazards of tall buildings appearing out of the snow, and they stayed close together, one slightly beneath the other, so as not to lose sight of one another. Their powerful wings settled into an easy rhythm that they could have maintained for countless hours, but even so, it soon became apparent to them that they would have to choose some other means of travel. The snow was driving into their eyes and blinding them, and the winds up there were gusty and erratic, and made them swirl and spiral in a way that made it almost impossible to stay close together. On several occasions they lost sight of each other, and had to circle and call until they met up again. It was possible for them to continue on, but it would be a slow and anxious journey.

The suburbs of the city were beneath them. The two birds passed quickly over a sprawling area of housing estates, then followed the line of the main road towards the centre of the city. It might have been the instinct of the birds to take refuge on the water, or it might have been an unrealised decision which their human minds had reached, but there was no doubt now about their destination. They were heading for the river.

As they came closer to the city centre and the buildings and traffic became more dense, Tess and Kevin could feel the slight rise in temperature. All those houses and offices were heated, and all the cars were burning fuel, and the excess heat was rising into the air. The snow seemed a little softer. It slid off their wings without sticking at all, and it didn't sting their eyes so badly. Nonetheless, it was a great relief when, surprisingly soon, the broad band of the river came into sight.

Tess was flying a little ahead of Kevin, and below him, but he was within her field of vision constantly. All of a sudden, there was a wobble and a flutter of darkness where he had been, and then she was on her own in the swirling snow. She wheeled in a great arc and turned back to see a black drake with a green head flapping towards her as fast as its little wings would carry it. Tess understood. Two albatrosses landing on the Liffey would undoubtedly cause a little more attention than they wanted.

The long spell of cold weather had caused parts of the river to freeze over, even before the snow had started to fall, but a channel through the middle had been kept clear by the current for most of its length. If anyone had been watching, they wouldn't have been too surprised to see two ducks coming in to land and floating along downstream for a while. They would have been a little more surprised, however, to see both ducks dive, one after another, and not come up again.

High above the Polar ice cap, Lieutenant Andy

'Scud' Morgan was flying a medium-range bomber with a full complement of armed missiles. The plane was on loan from the Pakistan Air Force, who had bought it from its manufacturers in the USA some nine months earlier. He checked the radio link with ground control to make sure that he wasn't being overheard, then he said: 'At least it doesn't smell of curry.'

'Huh?' said his co-pilot, Mark Hadders, who was sitting in the seat behind him.

'No garlands round the control panel. No incense burning under the seats.'

'Huh?' said Hadders again. He was cleaning his fingernails with a tooth broken from a pocket comb. The comb had about twelve teeth left. Scud Morgan hated Mark Hadders more than anyone on earth. He hated Mark Hadders more than he hated the Russians or the Iraqis or even the Cubans. Mark Hadders was a numbskull. Scud didn't know where he had got the nick-name 'Squash', but he was willing to take a good guess. The only part of Hadders' brain that worked was the bit that handled the aeroplane. The rest of it was completely atrophied.

But he had to talk to somebody. 'They didn't use the plane to clear some of their homeless off the streets,' he said, more loudly than he needed to.

'Why should they?' said Hadders. 'We don't. Besides, I think they're mostly Muslims in Pakistan. They don't go in for the incense and garlands stuff.'

'Dumb asshole,' muttered Morgan.

'Huh?'

'I said, "some hell-hole". Down there.' He pointed down at the floor of the cockpit beneath his feet.

They were flying above the storms, in bright sunshine. Beneath them there was nothing but unbroken cloud for mile after mile after mile.

'Anything on the radar, Jake?' said Morgan. The technician was behind them in the body of the plane, dozing over a bank of specially installed surveillance equipment. 'Couple of planes,' he said. 'That's all.'

'Theirs or ours?' There was no answer, so he said: 'Ha ha. Theirs or ours. Joke.'

There was still no answer. Hadders had finished cleaning his nails and was reading another of those dumb books that he seemed to go through like comics. Morgan had tried one once, but it made no sense at all. It was by some British woman who had been dead for a hundred years and whose brain had been dead for a hundred and fifty.

'They think we're crazy, you know?' he said.

Hadders sighed and rested his book on his knee. 'Who, Andy?'

'The Pakistanis, the Israelis, everyone who's cleaning up by hiring our own airplanes back to us.'

'No they don't, Andy.'

'Sure they do. And they're right, aren't they? We got sixteen hundred planes in the air, day and night, dodging each other like a swarm of mosquitos, and what are we fighting? A snowstorm.'

'Don't worry about it, Andy. We're not doing anybody any harm. Let them think what they like.' He picked up his book again.

'But I wasn't trained to not do anybody any harm!' said Morgan. 'I wasn't trained to spend eight hours a day pretending to be a weather satellite!'

'Come on,' said Hadders. 'Look around you, Andy. The sun is shining in a clear blue sky. At least we're not down there wearing snow goggles and dodging polar bears.'

'Anything would be better than this,' said Morgan. 'Sitting up here and getting bed sores on my rear end with some lunatic who reads . . . what do you call that stuff, anyway?'

'Literature,' said Hadders.

'Hell, that ain't literature!' said Morgan. 'Literature is what they give you when you can't decide which hi-fi system to go for. I got piles of it at home.'

Hadders wasn't listening. He was mentally absent again, reading his book.

'Anything new, Jake?' said Morgan.

'Couple of planes,' said Jake.

CHAPTER SIXTEEN

Goats had the secret of mischievous fun, it was true, but the spirit of pure joy had been perfected by another species and made its own. Two of these creatures were now speeding down the River Liffey, keeping well below the surface except when they had to rise, briefly, to catch air. They were dolphins, and they were heading for the open sea.

There are other sea creatures as fast as dolphins, but there are none that enjoy their speed so much. There are other sea creatures that live among their own kind, but there are none that take so much pleasure in each other's company. And on land or sea, there are no creatures anywhere that get such enjoyment out of merely being alive.

Tess and Kevin sped downstream, catching the strongest currents to help them on their way. They stayed close together, weaving around bridge supports, making small detours to get a quick look at interesting bits of wreckage on the river bed. There were prams, bicycles, supermarket trolleys, there were sunken boats, and cars, and once they passed a bus, with its rows of silted windows gazing vacantly towards the surface.

Tess knew that if she had to choose now, she would not be a cat. There was nothing that compared with being a dolphin. Her awareness was acute, her intuition sharp, and her body flowed with the current, all comfort and sinuous strength. If there had been time, she would have stood on her tail in the water and laughed at the people crossing O'Connell Bridge or walking to work beside the river. She would have done it not because she wanted their attention and applause, but because joy, more than anything else in the world, is for sharing.

Many, many miles away, between Norway and Iceland, the nearest krool was sliding towards them along the top of the rapidly expanding ice cap. It knew nothing of dolphins, and nothing of joy. All it knew was cold, and an endless, relentless hunger.

From above, the krools were invisible. They were round and shallow, roughly the shape of an upturned saucer, and so huge that they could cover an average-sized town without leaving any trace of it. Because they were very much colder than the snow around them, it didn't melt when it landed on their backs, but gave them a coating of camouflage. So perfectly did they blend into the surrounding snowfields that they could not be seen at all, even when they were moving, unless you happened to be right in front of them.

And if you were, you were in big trouble. For krools will stop at nothing when the time comes around to expand their icy kingdom across the globe. They will slide over land or sea on the carpet of ice that they spread for hundreds of miles before them with their snowy breath, and as they travel they will eat anything of animal or vegetable origin which lies beneath the snow or above it. Trees, rocks, houses, and all the ice and snow which cover them, are swept into the great maw of the krool and processed by its phenomenal digestive system. It sifts out what is useful and discards what is not as a powdery mixture of ground ice and stone. And the more it eats, the larger and colder it becomes.

The only enemy the krool fears is heat. Even a small animal which might somehow survive the vanguard storms by burrowing a hole in the snow can cause a reaction of revulsion in the krool as it passes over, and give it a spell of indigestion. The heat of the drilling rig had enraged the krool who encountered it, and caused it to heave and shudder for several days before it regained its strength and went on.

Such instances, however, are rare. The krools give fair warning of their arrival, and those warm-blooded creatures who are unable to keep pace ahead of the storms are usually frozen corpses by the time the krools arrive.

At the mouth of the River Liffey, Tess and Kevin turned east into the Irish sea, then northwards up the coast. They stayed close to the shore, where the water was warmer, but even so it soon became clear that they would need more insulation than they had to cope with the cold seas ahead of them. There was only one possibility for a journey as long as the one they were about to undertake and, reluctant as they were to change out of dolphin form, they knew that they would have to.

The oceans, as any seaman will testify, exist in a different part of time from the land. If anyone were to ask Tess how long her journey through the Irish Sea and up into the Norwegian Straits took her, she would have been unable to answer. How long is an hour? An hour doing homework or an hour at the fun-fair or an hour when you're too sick to go out and play? How long is an hour for a whale? For the whole of that trip beneath the waves, time was a currency without value, as meaningless as pound coins are to a frog.

Tess's human mind was all but engulfed by the phenomenal intelligence of the whale, and it was as much as she could do to keep her purpose intact. Whales have a knowledge of the whole global ocean with its varying currents and temperatures and moods, not as a person remembers some place where they have been, but as they might know their own house or garden, without ever having to think about it. But more than that, they could know each part of their immense home and what was happening there, even though they were not in it, for the voices of whales travel far and their thoughts travel further.

This much Tess might have been able to remember, but it was only the tattered and tawdry edge of the truth, the way that words can only explain the edges of dreams and not their vivid depths. The whole of that world could not be held in the limited mind of a human being, and was lost to her for ever when the time came to leave the oceans behind. But the thing that Tess never forgot was the whales' code of honour. For the whales know the ways of the ocean from top to bottom and from end to end, and that means that they know where the whaling boats lie. It is not stupidity which makes whales easy prey for the gunners, but their knowledge that the ocean is their own, and that it is better to die than to move even by the width of a flipper towards the faint-hearted existence of the hunted.

Krools move with astonishing speed when they first wake up. The areas of the planet which are near the polar regions have no resistance to their advance, because they are affected by the presence of the krools even as they sleep. They are territories which are already claimed by the cold and merely need to be re-established.

As they move towards the equator, however, their progress slows, partly because they come into contact with the sun. By the time these krools had reached the line of sixty-five degrees latitude, which runs through the middle of Norway and Sweden, and through Siberia, Alaska and North Canada, they were already slowing down. Their snowstorms still preceded them by hundreds of miles, but would spread more slowly as they blew towards Southern Europe and the USA.

The krools on the Norwegian Sea were having a particularly hard time of it. They had long since passed the limit of permanent pack ice and were having to use enormous reserves of cold to freeze the surface of the sea before them as they went. It was a hungry time for them as well, because there was no nourishment to be had from the sea, whose citizens stayed well below the freezing surface. All krools are dangerous, but a hungry krool is the most dangerous of all.

CHAPTER SEVENTEEN

When Tess and Kevin reached the fresh edge of the ice cap, now lying between Iceland and Norway, they said goodbye to the world of the whales and turned themselves into seals for their re-emergence on to the surface.

Despite their layer of blubber, they were shocked by the intensity of the cold. Snow was still falling, but it was a very different kind of snow from the large, soft flakes which were still settling on Dublin. Here the particles were small and dense, as though the air itself were ice that had lost its solidity but nothing of its coldness. It froze their whiskers as soon as they flopped out of the sea, and it stung their nostrils and eyes.

Tess stood beside Kevin, both of them blinking against the swirling snow and wondering what to do. Her mind searched for possibilities, but there were only two. To turn back, or to go on. It was Kevin who made the decision. He touched her nose briefly with his, and began to shuffle himself forwards. Tess followed.

But seals are cumbersome on land, and unhappy. Their exertions warmed them but they were making little headway. After a while they stopped to rest, but as soon as they did, the cold began to bite into them again. So they moved on in a more effective manner, as polar bears this time.

Tess was torn between conflicting instincts. She wanted to turn back, to the solid safety of whales and dolphins and home, but at the same time she was afraid of being separated from Kevin in this white and terrifying world. She knew that nothing would persuade him to give up, even though she had long ago forgotten the feeling that had made her understand why. She had the awful sensation of being caught up in his life, his search for some intangible thing which she neither understood nor wanted. It made her feel helpless and worthless, with no choice but to trail along in his tracks and accept whatever was going to happen.

And there was only one thing, as far as she could see, that could happen. They would walk into the snow and ice until they could walk no longer, and then they would die. She wondered what had happened to the other polar creatures, the bears and Arctic foxes with their silver coats, and she hoped that at least some of them had managed to stay on land and keep ahead of the storms. She shuddered and shook a crust of snow from her coat. Her fur was thick, but not thick enough, she knew, to protect her for much longer.

Kevin was still walking with silent determination, but the snow was getting deeper as they got further from the edge of the ice, and it was soft and powdery, which made progress slow and tiring. Tess's eyes and lungs were sore from the bitter air. She dropped her head. White bears, white snow, white air constantly moving around them. The only change in all that whiteness was when, from time to time, Kevin turned around to make sure she was there, and then she saw his black nose and eyes.

It was almost a relief when night began to fall. To Tess, numb with cold and exhaustion, it no longer seemed to matter what form rest might take, as long as it came soon.

Kevin stopped. Directly in front of them was a miniature mountain, an iceberg which had been captured and imprisoned by the spread of the krools' carpet. Some of its facets were too sheer for snow to lodge there, and the ice showed through, darkly opaque, like crystal. To Tess it represented an obstacle, but to Kevin it was a godsend. Because around its base the snow had gathered into wide, deep drifts. He began to dig.

In the middle of the night, Tess woke. It was absolutely dark in the snowhole. If any moon or starlight filtered through the clouds above, it failed to make its way through the tunnel they had dug and into their tiny cave.

It was surprisingly, luxuriously warm in there, from the trapped heat of their furry bodies. Tess would have stretched if there had been room, but they had made the space just big enough for the two of them to sleep curled up, so that they wouldn't have to warm any extra air. She yawned and turned over so that she was facing Kevin, and now she realised why she had woken. It was a long time, who knew how long, since she and Kevin had talked together, and she wanted to do it now before daylight came and urged them into action. She Switched, and immediately felt a little frightened to be lying in total darkness with a large bear. She could smell bear fur and bear breath, and before it frightened her any further, she reached out and tugged at Kevin's thick, warm coat.

He started, then grew rigid, and then the coat between her fingers was cotton, a little damp.

'You idiot, Tess! Don't ever do that again!'

'What? What did I do?'

'I was a bear, you fool. You woke me up. I nearly ripped out your throat!'

'Wow.'

'I only just remembered in time!'

'Sorry,' said Tess.

Kevin said nothing, but turned awkwardly in the cramped space until he was on his back. Tess was afraid that she was going to cry and, as if he realised, he reached out his hand and touched her arm.

'It's OK,' he said. 'I shouldn't have shouted. I'm sorry.'

Tess turned so that she was on her back as well and their shoulders were squeezed tight against each other in the dark. For a long time they lay in silence breathing the warm, foetid air.

Tess's mind was a jumble. She knew that the most sensible thing to do was to turn back and go home, but she couldn't say it to Kevin. It would seem like a betrayal after they had come so far. And if they weren't going to go back, what did you say to someone when it might be your last conversation with them? There was an awful sense of the executioner's cell about the snowhole. And despite all they had been through together, Kevin seemed like a stranger again, lost in his own thoughts. But it was he who spoke first.

'What did she mean, Tess?'

'Who? Lizzie?'

'Yes. About what isn't?'

'I don't know.'

'But what could she have meant? It must have been important or she wouldn't have said it.'

'I don't know if that follows,' said Tess. 'Lizzie said an awful lot of things that weren't important.'

'Oh, come on, Tess. You're not going to start backing off again, are you? It's hardly time for it, you know.'

'Maybe it is the time for it. Maybe it's the only time. The last chance we have.' She expected him to be angry, but his answer was surprisingly calm.

'No, it's too late for that now. We've come this far because we believed what Lizzie said. It'd be completely pointless to give up now, just when we're getting to the heart of it.'

'The heart of what?'

Kevin shrugged, and they were squeezed so tightly together that Tess's shoulder rose with his. At another time she would have laughed, but at that moment laughter seemed to belong to a different life.

'Of what we are, I suppose,' said Kevin. 'Of survival, of freedom, of independence.' He sighed. 'But I don't know what the problem is. My mind feels as if it's shot through with steel cables, or something. Whenever I try to think about anything a bit different, like what isn't, I just find myself running along the same old lines. I can't seem to get anywhere.'

'I suppose we haven't done too badly so far,' said Tess, 'and most of the things we've done have been your ideas. The dolphins and the seals and the polar bears and this hole in the snow.'

'Yes. But it's all practical stuff, isn't it? It's all what is and not what isn't. But the polar bears aren't going to take us much further, are they? We couldn't last much longer out there, and we can't hole up for ever, either. We need something else now. Some leap of imagination.'

He fell silent again. Tess noticed that her eyes were flicking around in the darkness, seeking something to rest upon. She closed them, and must have dozed for a moment, because Kevin's voice woke her from a dream.

'Have you got your watch on?'

For some reason the dream was important, but when she tried to remember it, it slipped away from her. It was all snow, anyway, ancient and endless. She felt her wrist. 'Yes.'

'Has it got the date on it?'

Tess was already looking at it. 'It says seven-thirty,' she said, 'but I suppose the time is different up here. I can't see the date. That bit isn't luminous. Why do you want to know, anyway?'

'I was just wondering when my birthday was. It must be quite soon.'

'What date is it?'

'The thirtieth. Can't be that far off now.'

Suddenly Tess realised why he was asking. She had an awful image of Kevin losing the ability to change and being stuck out there in the frozen wastes. He would freeze in no time in that stupid parka. He didn't even have gloves. And going back would be just as dangerous. He might be in the middle of the sea when it happened, or up in the air. It was important to know.

'Haven't you got a match?' she said.

'Good thinking,' said Kevin, fumbling in his pocket.

The first match he struck hurt their eyes so much that they couldn't see the watch. As the second one was burning down, Tess held the watch up close to it.

'The twenty-eighth,' she said.

Just before the flame died, she caught the look of dismay in Kevin's face. Their situation seemed even more hopeless than before, if that was possible. But Kevin said: 'Never mind.'

'Never mind?'

'I was just thinking we might have had a bit of a party, that's all. But we'll have to skip it.'

'A party? Are you out of your mind?'

'No. It's part of the tradition, apparently. The girl who told me about it had one. I didn't really know her very well. She wasn't like you. But she invited me to her party, and I went. The day before her fifteenth birthday.'

'Why the day before?'

Kevin laughed. 'You can't very well throw a party if you're an eagle, can you?'

'An eagle?'

'Yes. She was into discos and motorbikes and stuff. An eagle suited her, actually. It was her kind of thing.'

'You mean . . . You mean you can choose?'

'Of course!' said Kevin. 'Didn't you know that? Whatever you are at the time of your birthday, that's what you stay. You can't Switch any more, that's all. But there's nothing to say you have to be human.'

Tess stared into the darkness, trying to take it in.

'I've spent months worrying about it,' Kevin went on. 'Ironic, isn't it? Months trying to choose between a rat and a sparrowhawk and an otter, and now it looks as if I won't have a choice at all when it comes down to it. I'll just have to take whatever I get.'

'No, Kevin,' said Tess. 'We could still get back.'

'How?'

'Somehow. I don't know.'

'I don't see how we could. But in any case, I don't seem to be too worried about it. I can't understand it, really, but ever since Lizzie said what she did, about us having more power than we know, I've had this kind of faith. I'm not worried about those things any more. They don't seem to matter.'

'But you can't just end up as a polar bear or a walrus! You're human, Kevin, you have to be human!'

He laughed again, and Tess felt her heart fill with despair.

'Why?' he said.

But she couldn't tell him. She couldn't explain that she wanted to dress him up and take him into a French restaurant, or that she would welcome him any time she got off the bus and found him waiting. Even if her pride would allow it, it made no sense out here, with the Arctic gales blowing all around them.

'I never was any good at being human,' he said. 'Even with my family, even before I knew what I was.'

'Why not?'

'I don't know. I just didn't have the knack. My brother did. He was older than me, and he got along OK with everyone. My father's a toolmaker, and he does a lot of work at home. Makes all kinds of bits and pieces that people want. My brother was always out in his workshop with him, helping him. But I couldn't take an interest in it. I always got everything wrong, no matter how hard I tried.'

'So what? That doesn't mean anything.'

'It did, though. It meant that I didn't fit in with the men in the family, you see. And my mother . . .' He stopped.

'What about your mother?'

'I don't know quite how to explain it. She was always there, always. She never had a job, she never went anywhere, she was there every day when I came home from school and she did all the things that mothers are supposed to do. But in another way she wasn't there at all. She wasn't there for me. Her mind was always on something else, on what she was doing or on what she was listening to on the radio, or on something that she kept locked away inside herself somewhere.'

Tess noticed that the snow cave wasn't as warm as it had been. The cold seemed to be creeping through her from below, and she turned on to her side to relieve the discomfort in her back.

'When I look at it now,' Kevin went on, 'I see that she just didn't have it, that thing, whatever it is, that attention that people give to each other. I don't blame her for it. But at the time I used to think it was my fault, that I just wasn't good enough to be worth bothering with. But then I got angry about it, and it worked, because at least when I was bad she took some notice of me. That was around the time I discovered I could turn into a rat. It was ages before I discovered that I could be other things as well. In those days I used to set off for school in the mornings and spend the day with the other young rats, and even when my parents knew I was playing truant, there was nothing they could do to stop me. If they left me to the school in the morning, I'd slip off somewhere at break and do a bunk. The other kids hated me because I was different, and I hated them because they weren't.'

'I know the feeling,' said Tess.

'Yes. And as time went by I stopped bothering to go home. When I did turn up from time to time, they used to get into this awful flap and talk about borstals and reform schools, so I thought it was best to just stay out of the way.'

'Did you never spend time being human then, after that?'

'Oh, yes. I still turned up for their birthdays and Christmas, things like that. After a while they just accepted it and stopped asking questions. And I told you I spend . . . spent a lot of time in libraries. Sometimes I'd meet someone on the way and hang around with them for a while. But I never had a real friend. Not until . . .'

'Until what?'

'Phew. It's getting cold in here, isn't it?'

'Yes. We're not as warm as the bears were. What were you going to say just now?'

'It doesn't matter.'

Tess rested her head on the crook of her elbow. She was colder than she had realised, and beginning to feel drowsy again. She knew that it was dangerous. She remembered reading about it, about how the cold sends you off to sleep, and then you never wake up again. For a while she resisted and pulled herself awake to listen to Kevin's steady breathing in the darkness. What if they both fell asleep here? No one would ever find them. If the weather changed and the ice melted, their bodies would slide into the sea and be lost for ever. The thought of all those fathoms of dark water beneath them filled her with horror, but also a strange sort of resignation. They were so small in the middle of all this. Air, water, ice, and nothing else for hundreds of miles. Suddenly, there was no more resistance. She allowed her mind to drift away wherever it wanted, and there was a deep, deep sense of comfort.

The forgotten scene from the earlier dream returned. It was a landscape as bitter as the one outside their snow hole, but there was something moving across it, some kind of animal. And suddenly, Tess was wide awake.

'Kevin!'

He jumped at the urgency in her voice and she knew that he, too, had been asleep. 'What?'

'I've got it! All that stuff about what isn't.'

'Have you?'

'Yes. It's so simple, I can't believe we didn't think of it before.' She was determined to stay awake now, and she sat herself up so that the top of her head was wedged against the roof. 'Lizzie was right. We're completely caught up in the things around us, just trying to copy what already exists. But what about something that used to exist, and doesn't any more?'

Kevin was holding his breath, and Tess could feel his sense of excitement. 'Go on,' he said.

'Well, what about when there really was an ice age? There were animals that lived in those times, weren't there?'

'What, like dinosaurs?'

'Yes. Except that the dinosaurs didn't make it. They didn't adapt. But some other creatures did.

Kevin let out his breath with a gasp. 'Mammoths!' he said.

'Exactly! I saw them, Kevin, just now in a sort of dream. Walking through the snow. And why shouldn't we? I'm sure we could. We know what they looked like. I'm positive we could get a feel for them.'

'Of course we could. It'd be a lot easier than a whale.'

There was no more to be said, and they fell silent, their minds full of new hope. After a while, Tess said: 'Kevin?'

'Yes?'

'We ought to be bears again. Until the morning. It's too cold in here. It's dangerous.'

'Yes, you're right,' he said, but he didn't Switch, and Tess had a feeling that he was waiting for something. 'Don't go to sleep again,' she said.

'No. I'm not. I was just thinking.'

'What?'

'Well, if I got stuck as a mammoth. If my birthday came.'

Tess said nothing, thinking about it, and he went on: 'I know there's nothing you could do about it. I wouldn't ask you to stay with me or anything. But maybe you could . . . I don't know, just keep an eye on me somehow. So I wouldn't be completely alone.'

'Of course I would, Kevin. I'd do anything. I'd go to the ends of the earth if I had to.'

'I know you would,' he said, and then he laughed. 'You already have, in a way, haven't you?'

Tess's pride reared up. 'I didn't come here just because of you, you know,' she said.

'I know that,' said Kevin. 'But you're still the only friend I ever had.'

Before she could answer, he was a bear again and, with a sigh, she joined him.

CHAPTER EIGHTEEN

The two mammoths moved slowly but solidly across the snowfields. Their long, woolly coats provided perfect insulation against the blizzards, and their shaggy eyebrows and whiskery nostrils protected them from the effects of the freezing air. So little heat escaped through all that insulation that snow landing on their backs didn't melt, and even provided a further layer of protection.

It also provided a partial shield against the sensitive infra-red scanners in the planes that passed from time to time above their heads.

'Anything new, Jake?'
'Naa.'

They were flying low this time, through the white heart of the blizzard. There was little or no danger of encountering anything in the air. The high points in the pack ice were well charted, and their radar screens would give warning well in advance of anything that might be in their path, but even so, Scud found it nerve-wracking to be flying so totally blind.

'That freighter out of the way?'

'What freighter?'

'You said there was a freighter.'

'Hell,' said Jake, 'that was an hour ago. He'll be over Stockholm by now.'

'Nothing else?'

'No. Wait a minute, though.'

'What?'

Even Hadders put down his book for a moment.

'Nothing. Infra-red's just picking up a couple of animals down below. Small ones. I don't know how they can survive down there.'

'Poor suckers,' said Hadders.

'Poor suckers?' said Scud. '*They're* poor suckers? What about us?'

The only danger that the mammoths were aware of was hunger. There was no source of food for miles around, not even the rough Arctic vegetation on which they had learned to survive in the past. Their reserves of fat would keep them going for a while, but for how long they didn't know. It took a lot of energy to keep those massive bodies warm, and a lot more to keep them moving.

But keep moving they did. Tess and Kevin had passed another test. Kevin's faith had held, even if Tess's hadn't, and circumstances had proved him right. The mammoths were slow but they were comfortable, and they were making steady progress towards the north.

The hours passed. The human parts of their minds chafed at the tedium of the changeless landscape, but the mammoths had learnt patience over the generations, and plodded along tirelessly.

The krool sensed them coming long before they were able to see it, and its small, uncomplicated brain went into a momentary seizure. For although it was a poor thinker, its memory was as long and as ancient as its life, and it was well acquainted with mammoths. The prospect of encountering these two was not a pleasant one.

A dead mammoth is an agreeable snack for a krool, but a live one is a different proposition entirely. This particular krool had once had the experience of swallowing a whale which had been trapped beneath the ice, unable to breathe and dying. Its phenomenal internal temperature had crippled the krool, and it had never forgotten the agonizing days that followed as it battled with the heat the way a person battles with infection. Even two live mammoths would not be as bad as that, but they would nevertheless create a considerable disturbance in its system, and it would have to lie up for a while until they were digested.

In the normal course of events, a krool would not even consider eating a mammoth, which was one of the reasons why the mammoths had come to survive their last colonisation of the earth. A krool encountering a mammoth in the usual course of events would flatten the leading edge of its mantle so that the mammoth wouldn't know it was there and would merely continue on its way, traversing the krool's back until, after a few hours, it reached the other side. If this particular krool had not been so hungry, it would have left the two mammoths to go along their way. But it could not allow any source of food to escape, even if it caused a belly-ache. It lay still and waited.

Some miles away, Scud Morgan's bomber had completed an in-flight refuelling operation and started its return journey. In a few more hours it would make a radio-controlled landing on the salted runway of an air base in central England and its crew would get out of their air-bound prison.

Jake was dozing. Hadders was reading. Scud was flying as low as he dared, for the sake of producing adrenalin.

Tess and Kevin blundered straight into the waiting krool. One moment there was nothing ahead of them except untrodden snow and the next, a whole section of it lifted and towered above them, and they were gazing with horror at the black underbelly of the krool. For an instant, Tess thought that the world had collapsed and she was staring into nothingness, a gaping abyss. Then she saw the eye. A single, huge, unblinking eye, gelid and green, looking straight at her.

If Lizzie had been wrong, it would have been the end, not only of the two mammoths, but of Tess and Kevin as well. For the mantle was above them now and the huge, cavernous maw was opening as the krool pushed forward to swallow its prey. But if Lizzie had been wrong she would not have sent the two young Switchers out to test their strength against the krools. Lizzie knew, and quicker than thought, Tess knew too, that they did indeed have powers beyond their wildest dreams. Kevin had been right. If they hadn't been faced with the ultimate test of their skills, they might never have learned them. Because, if there had been time for thought, Tess would never have believed that what happened next was possible. The krool's mantle was dropping like a monstrous fly swatter. Not even a bird would have had the speed to dodge out from under it. But Tess Switched, quicker than she had ever Switched before, and suddenly the krool was rearing away again and backing off.

For Tess's heart had understood even more clearly than her mind what Lizzie meant by being what isn't. And it had acted before her mind had been able to doubt, and to stop it. In front of the krool's retreating underbelly was a huge and magnificent dragon, and then there were two of them, blasting flame at the hideous eye, which shrivelled and melted and dripped like warm treacle into the snow. The krool reared as high as it could go, a mile into the sky, but the dragons took to the wing and continued their pursuit until it collapsed and doubled back on itself like a monstrous, black pancake.

The two dragons leapt for the skies in a delirium of delight. They were faster, cleverer, more powerful than any creature on earth, and they swooped and soared, chased each other's tails and tumbled in the air in sheer elation. This was the feeling that their premonitions had promised them, the certainty of power beyond human imagination, the sensation of absolute freedom. For all the elements were theirs to enjoy. They were equally at home in water, earth and air, but they were not bound by any of them. They carried the secret of fire within them, and even the great ice wastes all around them could cause them no discomfort. They were the rulers of all they surveyed, and there was no creature on earth that could defeat them.

In the midst of their celebrations, they heard the plane passing above them in the clouds. Heard it first, and then saw it, with their infra-red vision.

Just as it saw them. The scanner beeped, warning of a strong signal. Jake sat bolt upright and stared at the screen.

'You got something, Jake?' said Scud.

'Holy God,' said Jake. 'What the hell is that?'

'What is it, Jake, what is it? You got something?' Hadders sat up and turned around in his seat.

'I've never seen anything like it,' said Jake, his eyes filled with wonder.

'What the hell is it, Jake?' Scud yelled.

Jake moved into military mode, sharp and efficient. 'We got hotspots, boys. Two of them. I don't know what they are and I don't know where they came from, but they're like nothing I ever saw before.'

Hadders had left his seat and was standing in the small space beside Jake, looking over his shoulder at the screen. 'Swing around, Scud,' he said. 'We're losing them.'

'Who's giving the orders around here?' screamed Scud. 'What the hell are you doing, standing back there telling me what to do?'

'You should see this, sir. We should get a better look before we go past.'

Scud gritted his teeth and swore, but he dipped his wings and swung around in the tightest circle the plane could handle. 'Come in, base,' he said into the radio mike. 'This is Delta Zero Five, are you reading me?'

General Wolfe was sitting at his desk in Mission Control when one of the technical assistants called him over to the computer terminal which was receiving Scud Morgan's pictures. 'God damn,' he said. 'What the hell is that?'

'Damned if I know,' said the aide. 'There's no plane in the world that flies like that.'

The shapes on the screen were descending in rapid circles, leaving a residue of heat in their wake that showed up on the monitor like the tail of a comet. The plane was passing above them and moving away again.

'Get on to the guys in that plane,' said Wolfe. 'Tell them to stay above those things and keep sending back pictures.'

'Yes, sir.'

By now there was quite a gathering around the terminal, watching the screens. 'I knew it,' said Wolfe. 'Didn't I tell you, huh? I knew there was something in there.'

CHAPTER NINETEEN

The plane above their heads was unsettling, but dragons are not easily intimidated. When they realised that it was not going to go away, they agreed to ignore it and go in search of more krools. They split up, one going east and the other west, flying low enough to be able to see the ground beneath them.

The plane above circled one last time, then followed Kevin. For a while he allowed it to drone along behind him, but then he grew irritated by it, and doubled back on himself, too rapidly for the plane to follow. Then he flew south at top speed for a while, and did not turn back to his original course until he was sure that the skies around him were clear.

Scud Morgan swore. Jake shook his head. Mark Hadders went back to his seat and his book.

A krool in a snowstorm is not easy to find, even for a dragon. Kevin scanned the ground as he flew, but it was only by chance that he came across his second krool. It was sliding southwards across Norway, more slowly now than in the preceding weeks, but still making good progress. It had fed well recently, cutting a great swathe through the forested regions in its path, and had grown to enormous dimensions.

Krools do not reproduce like most of the other creatures of the earth. They don't mate with others of their kind, and they produce neither eggs nor young. When they reach a certain critical mass, however, they divide, simply split down the middle and become two, like amoebae. Kevin was able to spot this krool from the air because it was in the process of doing just that.

Where it was splitting into two the camouflage of snow was shifting and revealing patches of the glutinous black flesh beneath. Kevin slowed, wheeled round and returned, spitting flame. But by the time he reached it, the krool had become aware of the hot little presence above and glued itself firmly to the ground.

The first krool had been so easy to dispose of that Kevin wasn't prepared for the battle which followed. The krool did nothing, merely sat tight, knowing that as long as it didn't reveal its underneath to the attacker it was almost invulnerable. Almost, but not quite. Kevin came in time after time, throwing flame constantly. Wherever he attacked the krool, it melted into black, oily liquid, but it was so huge that his best efforts made little impression on its bulk.

He stopped for a while, trying to work out a plan. It was tiring, the way he was acting, and he realised that he was using too much energy. If he became exhausted, he would have to rest, and then feed, and when he thought about feeding his mind became filled with pictures of what dragons best like to eat, which is people. And when he thought of people, he could think of only people that he knew, and he wondered if any Switchers before him had experienced the weird sensation of imagining a slap-up meal consisting of their relatives and friends.

To take his mind off these unpleasant thoughts, he returned to the krool and flew up the gradual contour of its body until he reached the highest point. Then he burned away in one spot, calmly and consistently, until he had produced a hollow full of bubbling black liquid like a cauldron. Still he carried on, until at last the heat melted a hole right through the krool and the liquid flowed away on to the ground beneath it. The beast began to convulse, flapping its skirts and heaving its great body so that the snow which covered it flew up in a thick cloud. Kevin hovered in the air and waited until the krool gave a final shudder and lay still.

High above, a satellite had picked up the heat emissions from the battle, and three planes were converging on the spot. But by the time they arrived, Kevin was gone, and their surveillance equipment picked up no signs of life.

But a few hundred miles away, above Greenland, another plane was about to intercept Tess's path. Her infra-red image had just appeared on the aircraft's monitor, and a rapid radio communication had put the crew on to the offensive. Wolfe didn't know what those things were out there, but he wasn't taking any chances. The first heat-seeking missile was armed and ready to go.

Tess's flight path was erratic and unpredictable, and the pilot of the bomber wasn't about to take chances. As soon as he got a clear radar fix, he fired off the missile and swung around out of the area.

Tess had known that the plane was there, but she hadn't expected that it would be able to detect her. She accepted her dragon ability to see objects by the heat they emitted, but she had no idea that there was an equivalent technology available to the military. So, when she picked up the image of the missile snaking towards her, she was completely off guard. If she had been expecting it she might have dodged, since dragons can perform fantastic aerial manoeuvres which no missile could possibly follow. Instead, instinctively, she changed herself into a swallow. The missile swept past, catching her in its current of air and swirling her around in the blizzard. Then, finding itself without a target, it ploughed blindly on, straight into the snow beneath.

The swallow was well clear of the centre of the explosion, but even so, chunks of snow and ice flew up to where she was recovering her balance high above. She flew upwards and away, but in no time at all the blood of the little bird began to freeze. She listened for a moment, and as soon as she was sure that the plane was not returning she Switched back into the warm and fearless form of the dragon.

The monitor in Mission Control slowly cleared and became blank as the heat from the explosion died away. A great cheer went up. General Wolfe leant back in his chair and clasped his hands behind his head in satisfaction. 'Whatever it was, we got it,' he said.

'Uh oh,' said a technician behind him. 'I'm afraid not, sir.'

'What?' Wolfe sat up again. There, on the screen,

was the hot spot again, as clear as ever. It was heading east with surprising speed. 'But it disappeared, didn't it?'

'It looked like it did,' said the technician. 'Maybe the heat from the explosion just masked it somehow. It's there now, anyhow.'

It was, and racing back through the snowstorms towards Kevin. He had heard Tess's call and was coming to meet her. From their positions all over the Arctic Circle, the military planes moved in.

It was nearly dark when the two dragons met above the Norwegian Sea, and it was time to call it a day. Their infra-red vision enabled them to see planes overhead, but no kind of vision would enable them to find krools in the dark. Kevin wanted to stay a dragon, but Tess had learnt that they were not as invisible as they had believed, and insisted on the safety of polar bears. Kevin capitulated. They dug in quickly and slept straight away, curled closely together for comfort.

As soon as the sun came up the next morning, the two hot spots were picked up on the monitors of a surveillance plane. They didn't appear gradually, as a plane does when it starts its engines and warms up, and they neither taxied to a runway nor rose vertically. One moment there was nothing on the infra-red screens above, and then there were two large, hot objects flying off at impossible speed in different directions.

This time, Tess and Kevin had a plan. It was a dangerous plan and would require all their courage and all their wits but, if it worked, it would be a brilliant way to get rid of the krools. All they had to do was to find them.

They had decided to fly low, so low that a krool would appear to them as a patch of slowly-rising ground which would then fall away again. In the middle of a blizzard such flying required steel nerves and lightening fast reactions, but the dragon has both, even at the speed of a jet plane.

When they had talked in the early hours of the morning, Tess and Kevin had agreed that there must be a vanguard of krools along the same latitude as the first ones they had found, to account for the even progress of the blizzards that preceded them. So the dragons flew in straight lines, due east and due west from where they had started. Several times in the first hour, Tess slowed and circled to examine a suspicious slope in the ground, but each time it was a false alarm. Above her the planes criss-crossed continuously, and she had already out-foxed three missiles before she found her first krool. As soon as she was certain of it, she rose some distance into the clouds above and circled steadily, waiting. Before long she saw the tell-tale heat of the approaching plane and heard its engine. As soon as it was within range, it launched its missile. Tess dived at full speed towards the unsuspecting krool. The missile spun after her, coming closer to her tail, until at the last minute, she Switched as she had done before and swung out of the way. It worked. The gathered momentum of the dragon dive flung the little bird out into the blizzard at terrifying speed, and away from the explosion. A few bits of exploded krool reached her as she shot through the air, but she was too busy trying to gain control of her dizzying flight to be concerned about them.

In Mission Control, the observers watched the clearing screen in tense silence. Then someone said: 'We got one this time.'

There was no cheer. This had happened before. 'Don't count your chickens,' said Wolfe, then groaned as the hot spot reappeared and resumed its eastward flight.

On the other side of Greenland, heading west, Kevin was playing the same game, with slightly more success. He had discovered a better way of finding his prey.

A krool crossing land leaves a distinct trail behind it where it has cut a mile-wide path through the vegetation and left nothing but a clean sweep of powdered snow, ice and rock. Kevin happened to notice this when he found his first krool of the day, and after that he stopped looking for their convex forms and searched instead for abrupt tree-lines or abnormally smooth stretches of snow. The method served him well. He found krool after krool, and each time he hovered above them and waited until the military arrived.

As the day wore on, General Wolfe grew increasingly exasperated. The events of the day were beginning to send shivers down his spine. It was becoming clearer all the time that whatever those things were, they were playing games with him. The phone was ringing from Washington a little too often and the questions were becoming embarrassing.

But the strangest thing of all was that whatever was happening out there was having the desired effect on the weather. Already the blizzards were dying out and clouds were disappearing from large areas that had previously been covered. In southern England and

Ireland, he was told, the sun was shining and the snow was beginning to melt.

It was just in time for Lizzie. For the first few days of the blizzards, Mr Quigley had been extremely helpful. He had come every day with whatever supplies Lizzie needed, and he and his daughter had shovelled the snow away from her door and made paths to Nancy's shed and the henhouse. But then, one day, he had come and told her that he had sold all his stock and managed to get a passage for himself and his family on a ferry to Cyprus, and he could not let the opportunity pass. He had brought her provisions for a fortnight and a hundredweight of rock salt to help against the snow, but beyond that he could do nothing more for her.

When the daily digging became too much for her, Lizzie brought Nancy and the hens into the house and let them have the use of the scullery. The mains water had long since frozen tight, so she filled the bath and the sink and a few old milk churns with snow. Then she brought in as many logs as she could stack in the hall, and closed the doors. She was dug in like an Arctic creature in her little snow-hole of a cottage, and was forgotten by the world.

The drifts rose until they covered the downstairs windows, and, since the power lines were down over half the country, Lizzie moved around in the dim light of the fire, saving her candles for emergencies. The first thing to run out was the oats she fed to Nancy and the chickens, and she had to start sharing her own rations with them. Then water began to get scarce. The plug in the bath had proved useless, and the snow which Lizzie had gathered so laboriously ran away as soon as it melted. She was reduced to scraping snow from the insides of the drifts outside the windows and melting it over the fire, and anyone who has ever tried this will know that it is a lot of work for very little return. By the time the sun appeared, Lizzie was exhausted, dispirited, and almost down to the last of her provisions.

If it hadn't been for the cats, she would probably not have known the snow had stopped until the next day. Her kitchen was as dark as a basement with the windows all covered in drifts, but it was too cold to sit upstairs where there was still light. The cats, however, went up and down quite often during the day to use the litter tray that Lizzie had set up in the spare room for them as soon as they could no longer get out.

It was when Moppet failed to return from one of these visits that Lizzie went upstairs to investigate and found him curled up on the windowsill in the sunshine. For the first time since Tess and Kevin had left her house, Lizzie's stiff old back straightened up. She went to the window, prised it open, and called out to the sky: 'You did it, you little horrors! You made it!'

CHAPTER TWENTY

Back at the edge of the Arctic Circle, the dragons were still at work. Tess had eventually discovered Kevin's method of detection for herself, and was making up for lost time.

In Mission Control, General Wolfe was getting fed up with throwing missiles at infra-red ghosts, but he had discovered that there was little else he could do. He had found volunteers to go in for close combat in fighter planes armed with machine guns and close-range missiles, but they had flown back bewildered. As soon as they came anywhere near to visual range, their targets disappeared. Simply vanished without trace.

Wolfe called them back. With outward confidence and inward despair, he continued with the missile attacks.

Tess and Kevin were in a mood of high exhilaration.

They were living by the skin of their teeth, dodging death one minute and tempting it the next. As a result, life had never seemed better or more precious.

And they were winning. Their phenomenal speed had taken them around the globe to meet again on the other side above Canada, where they played aerial tag and leapfrog together for a few minutes before turning round and starting back the way they had come, to pick off the krools they had missed.

Wolfe followed their progress on radar and infra-red. He now knew that he was playing into their hands in some way, but he also knew that the snow-storms were abating. He didn't know how he was going to explain it, but he was sure of one thing. He was going to take all the credit that was on offer when the time came.

The one in the west was circling again. 'Let him have it,' he said.

Fast as the dragons were, they couldn't make it back around the globe before nightfall. They could call to each other, though, and they did, before they came to land and settled as polar bears into their separate dug-outs for the night.

Tess slept fitfully, dreaming bear dreams and dragon dreams, and terrible dreams of Kevin trapped in the form of some awful creature for the rest of his life. A single bear produces very much less heat than two curled up together, and she woke before dawn, stiff and sore with the cold. She knew that the only way to get warm was to get moving, so she crawled out of the tunnel and was amazed to find herself standing in the middle of clearly visible snowfields, stretching away in all directions, glowing in the light of the stars which shone out of a cloudless sky.

A plane passed low over her head, blinking a single, white light. Tess shook her damp coat and began to trot northward.

In Mission Control, General Wolfe was popping caffeine pills to keep himself awake. The meteorological satellites were beaming down gratifying pictures of the cloud formations. A few isolated blizzards were still stretching southward like thick fingers, but otherwise the area below the line of seventy degrees latitude was clear.

But Wolfe knew that those things, whatever they were, would return in the daylight. He had spent most of the night in a fury of injured pride, and he wasn't about to give up. There were all kinds of theories buzzing around. Some said the hot spots were Iraqi war machines, developed for the purpose of freezing out the Northern Hemisphere and crippling the American and European economies. Others said they were UFOs making a bid to colonise the planet. Wolfe was willing to believe that they came from outer space, but nothing that had happened had succeeded in convincing him that they were not living beings of some kind. He hadn't forgotten those two tapes.

As Tess warmed up she began to make plans. The blizzards had died down, she knew, because of the krools she and Kevin had killed, but there would surely be others closer to the Pole which would need her attention. Even in the dark, however, she was reluctant to become a dragon now that the cover of clouds had gone, just in case some low-flying plane might get a sight of her in the starlight. So she Switched instead to a Canadian goose, and began to fly steadily north.

She was right about the krools. What she didn't know, however, was that they were no longer a danger. Apart from the unknown enemy in the skies, they were under increasing threat from their greatest enemy, the sun. Only in large numbers can krools be certain of producing sufficient freezing clouds to keep them covered and safe. A single krool cloud can be dispersed by warm winds and leave its maker helpless, melting in the sun. Already the second and third line of them were in rapid retreat, and the rearguard had retraced their tracks and slithered back into their icy beds.

Kevin woke at dawn, and the first thing he knew was that it was the day before his birthday. He had one more day and one more night.

He emerged from his den and stretched. It was still snowing, but the snow was softer that it had been, and kinder. He was feeling fresh, and ready for another day's action, but before that he wanted to have a look around, and he knew exactly how he was going to do it. In the blink of an eye he was a dragon again, moving rapidly up towards the top of the clouds.

The air force was waiting for him, and a passing plane let off a missile as he rose towards it, but he Switched and dodged it easily. It exploded beneath him, not far from his snow-hole. When he recovered his equilibrium, he Switched again, and set off at high speed towards the Pole. He flew so fast that he soon outdistanced the planes behind him, and by doubling and zig-zagging as he went, he was able to confuse the controllers on the ground until at last he found that he had a clear sky above him. Rapidly, he dropped a couple of hundred feet so that he could give himself the momentum he needed, then he launched himself like a rocket, straight up through the clouds and into the air above them.

It was similar to the way a spaniel will jump up above the long grass to get a look around, except that Kevin went up almost as far as the stratosphere. From there he could clearly see the pattern of clouds beneath, which told him the exact locations of the outlying krools. It took him scarcely a second to take it all in, and then he was dropping again, like a monstrous hawk plummeting down through the sky.

In front of the monitors in Mission Control, a dozen mouths dropped open in disbelief as radar relayed the astonishing feat.

'What the hell,' said General Wolfe, 'are we dealing with?'

Just across the Arctic Circle from Kevin, Tess had reached the safety of clouds and Switched. Kevin had been calling periodically throughout the morning and was delighted at last to get a reply. He called again, relaying his information about the whereabouts of the krools, and the two dragons set about finishing them off.

It was easy now. All they had to do was to sweep down along the fingers of cloud until they found the krools. After a while, Mission Control began to understand the pattern, and quite often the dragons found that the planes were already in position even before they arrived.

By late afternoon, Tess and Kevin had located every krool that lay outside the line of seventy degrees latitude. They met directly above the North Pole, where night had already fallen, to celebrate and discuss tactics. Kevin was full of the joys of victory, and was in favour of carrying on, but Tess wanted to stop and talk to him. She was as excited as he was, but for a different reason. For a while they argued in the air, until they became angry and began to burn each other's noses and ears with jets of flame, which sobered them up a bit. In the end, Kevin relented and they sprinted away from the planes gathering above them until they had left them behind. Then they geared down to geese in order to put the enemy off their tracks and flew on for a while. Finally, when the skies were clear of planes, they landed in a strange amphitheatre of ice in the middle of the Greenland Sea.

'Phew,' said Kevin, when they stood face to face at last. 'It's cold.'

'Yes,' said Tess. 'So we have to talk fast.'

'What's so important, anyway?'

'This,' said Tess. 'We've got the krools on the run, right?'

'Well, we've knocked most of them out, anyway.'

'Right. And I knocked out two today up in Northern Greenland that were definitely going backwards.'

'Did you?'

'Yes. Going at a hell of a speed, too. So listen. Maybe the job is finished, you know? And even if it isn't, I could always finish it off on my own if I had to.'

'But why should you?'

'Because maybe you can still have the chance to be what you want to be.'

'But there's not much choice up here, is there? Anyway, I quite like being a dragon.'

So did Tess, but if she had been a dragon at that moment, she would have burned his nose again. 'Don't be an idiot, Kevin,' she said. 'We've only survived so far because we can Switch! If you couldn't dodge those missiles and disappear at night you wouldn't stand a chance!'

Kevin sighed. 'I suppose you're right,' he said.

'But this way you still have a chance. With the speed we can travel as dragons, we could be in Ireland before morning. We might even have time for some bit of a party. At Lizzie's, maybe?'

'It's a bit risky, isn't it?' asked Kevin. 'They'll be able to follow us on radar, won't they?'

'So what?' said Tess. 'We've been dodging planes and missiles for two days, now. What could they possibly throw at us that we couldn't handle?'

Kevin said nothing. Tess rubbed her gloved hands together and blew on them. 'Come on, Kevin,' she said. 'It's too cold to stand around and think about it.'

'I suppose it is,' said Kevin. 'The only problem is, I still don't really know what I want to be. There was something nice about not having to choose, you know?'

'But you don't have to choose right now. You'll have all today and tonight to think about it. And in any case, you'll probably know when the time comes, won't you? The same way as you knew it was right to come up here?'

Kevin brightened. 'You know something?' he said. 'What?'

'For once in your life, you might be right.'

CHAPTER TWENTY-ONE

General Wolfe was on the edge of his seat. 'Come on, my tricky little friends,' he said to the moving blips on the monitor in front of him. 'You just keep right on going the way you are.'

The two UFOs were heading south, right out in the open above the Norwegian Sea. He had been following their progress for some time, watching the satellite pictures with growing anticipation. If they carried on in their present direction, they would soon be crossing the north-west tip of Scotland. And when they did, he would have a little surprise waiting for them.

At an air base in North Wales, Scud Morgan and his team were getting ready for take-off. They were in a line of planes similar to their own, crawling towards the runway, waiting their turn. The snow was still thick on the fields all around, but the skies were clear.

Scud was champing at the bit. 'Know something?' he said.

'Not a thing,' said Hadders, who was carefully checking over the instruments on the panel in front of him.

'I got a feeling we're going to see some action tonight.'

'I guess that's why they're sending us up there, Scud.'

'Yeah, course, I know that. But this feeling is more than that. It's in my bones, you know? Like, we were the first guys to spot those two aliens out there, weren't we?'

'I never saw any aliens.'

'What were they, then? They weren't planes. Everyone knows those two things weren't planes. You must be some kind of a nut-head if you think those two things are planes.'

'Nobody knows what they are,' said Hadders, 'and nobody knows how to stop 'em. But it seems to me that there's no sense in talking flying saucers here and getting ourselves into a stew.'

'A stew?' said Scud. He jammed on the brakes as he came up on to the tail of the plane in front, and the three of them lurched forward into their seat-belts. 'Who's getting into a stew? I'm not getting into a stew. Are you getting into a stew? Nobody gets into a stew in this bird, not as long as I'm in command, anyhow.'

Hadders sighed and continued with his last-minute checklist. 'All I'm saying,' Scud went on, 'is that I got this feeling. We were the first to see those two aliens, and I got an idea we're going to be the last.'

'Did you see any aliens, Jake?' said Hadders.

'Couple of planes,' said Jake.

There were no missiles aboard the bombers which lifted off, one after another into the star-lit sky. They were fully loaded though, but this time with another kind of weapon.

When Scud and his crew took off, Tess and Kevin were still well out over the Norwegian Sea. They were flying low, skimming close to the waves, enjoying their flight. The night air was clear and fresh, and they were beginning to believe that they had finally left the battlefield behind.

Once they had passed over the line of new ice that the krools had made, they got the occasional glimpse of a whale breaking the surface of the sea, and they knew that they were heading away from the cold, towards life again. Tess looked across at Kevin flying beside her, and it seemed that it was the first time she had been able to relax for days. What they had done was ridiculous, impossible. It made no sense at all, and yet it was true, and they had done it. The starlight shimmered from the metallic scales of Kevin's back as he turned to her and winked. She was a dragon, flying with another dragon across the sea beneath the stars, and she took time to drink it in and fix the images and sensations into her mind. Because she knew that whatever else happened, she would never feel like this again.

Within an hour, the thirty-five planes had reached their positions and were set in a holding pattern, waiting.

'You got a reading on them yet, Jake?' said Scud.

'Just what the satellite's sending.'

'They far off?'

'About fifteen minutes, I guess.'

'What's that on the radar, then?'

'Let's see. FT6R. That's Pete and Jeremy coming round again. Hi, guys.'

'Jeremy!' Scud spat. 'That's what you get for working with this British crowd. Whoever heard of a serviceman called Jeremy, for God's sake? Wouldn't you think he'd change his name or something? How can anybody fight a war when there's people called Jeremy flying around all over the place? How's a man supposed to think straight?'

'I'm not sure this is a war, Scud.'

'Read your book, Hadders. That's what some people do. Some people are born to read books and some are born to fight wars. I don't care what anyone else says, but when I'm in a plane, I'm fighting a war.'

Hadders broke one of the last spines from his comb and picked his teeth with it. 'You can say that again,' he said.

As the north tip of Scotland came into view, the two dragons did a quick loop-the-loop of delight. Wolfe, along with fifteen assembled advisers and assistants, held his breath. When the two UFOs resumed their course the print-outs on his table fluttered in the breeze.

They were over the land now, with the ragged western coast of Scotland to their right. Beneath them, the trees of huge forestry plantations poked their dark heads above the snow, and occasionally the sharp eyes of the dragons could make out the roofs of abandoned villages and isolated farmhouses. Tess was surprised to find that now and then she got a whiff of wood-smoke. There were people still surviving somehow, despite the depth of the snow. She was looking down, trying to get a glimpse of the heat of hearth-fires, and Kevin must have been as well, otherwise they would have not been taken so utterly by surprise by finding themselves flying straight into the path of an oncoming plane.

'They're going to pass right under us!' yelled Jake.

'And we're going to get 'em,' said Scud.

'OK,' said Hadders. 'Just take it easy, now. We all clear of other planes, Jake?'

'All clear. And we're on computer count-down, seven, six . . .'

'Hell, where are they? They got no lights or nothing.'

'Four, three . . .'

They were practically beneath the plane before they had time to blink.

'Two . . .'

Tess acted Goat, swung wildly to her left and upwards, Switching as she did so.

'One . . .'

But Kevin was just that little bit slower. He carried straight on, and he Switched, too.

'Zero!'

But he was too late. The napalm bomb dropped from the undercarriage of the plane and exploded in the air, scattering its flaming contents of sticky jelly through the sky and down on to the forest below.

'We got 'em!' yelled Scud. 'Did we get 'em, Jake, did we?'

'Get what?' said Hadders. 'I didn't see anything. Did you see anything?'

'I didn't see anything, but we sure as hell got 'em, whatever they were. Did we get 'em, Jake?'

'How should I know? I couldn't see anything.'

'But you got the machines. What do the machines say?'

'The machines say there's a big fire behind us, that's all.'

'Anything flying away from it?'

'Yeah. We are.'

'I knew it,' said Scud. 'I could feel it in my bones. We got 'em.'

Jake was still watching the satellite monitor in the back of the plane. 'I wonder,' he said.

'You bet we did,' said Scud. 'And you know something else?'

'What?' said Hadders.

'This is going to be cause for a celebration, pal. I'm going to buy you a brand new comb.'

By the time Tess had got control of her flight and swung round to see what was happening, the plane was gone and the forest was blazing. Above it, she could just make out a speck of flame which twisted as it tumbled down and was lost in the thick smoke and sparks which rose from the inferno beneath. Her bird mind was utterly calm and detached, but her human mind was screaming. 'Switch, Kevin, Switch!'

But it would have been no use. Nothing, not even the dragon, could have survived those flames. Kevin was done for.

Nonetheless she waited, an eagle hovering high above the forest as the fire reduced it to a skeleton of charred tree-trunks and melted the snow around its edges. She stayed long after the planes had stopped circling and gone away. She stayed until the dawn arrived, the dawn of Kevin's fifteenth birthday, but all it brought with it was military helicopters coming to examine the aftermath of the fire. They would find nothing.

With a heavy heart, Tess wheeled and flew away.

CHAPTER TWENTY-TWO

Tired and dispirited, Tess made her way back to Dublin. It was a difficult journey, and she tried several different birds before she finally settled on the Arctic tern. It was a tough little bird, she discovered, and coped well with the cold and the long hours on the wing, but even so, she was ready to drop by the time she spotted the Phoenix Park and came in to land.

The lights were on in her house. Tess stood among the trees across the street and looked around carefully. There was no one about. The snow was melting fast, but there were still deep drifts around the trunks of the trees and against hedges and walls. The prospect of warmth and rest was almost irresistible, but even as she made the Switch, Tess realised that something was wrong. Much as she loved her parents and longed for the comfort of home, what she needed above all else at this moment was understanding. The shock and grief she felt at Kevin's death struck her with full force now that she was human again, and it was something she would never be able to share with her parents. There was only one person in the world that she could tell, and that was Lizzie.

Reluctantly, Tess turned her back on the bright lights of her parents' house and returned to the shape of the brave little seabird. On tired wings she crossed the city and searched among the snowy fields and trees for the ruin of the big house and the little cottage beside it. When, after some time, she found it, she was relieved to see smoke rising from the chimney and paths cleared to the sheds. She landed on the roof of the hen-house and looked around for a while before she decided on the best way of getting into Lizzie's house without alarming her.

The other cats arched their backs and hissed when they heard the stranger come in through the cat-flap and scratch at the kitchen door, but Lizzie knew straight away.

'You's back!' she said as she opened the door. 'That was quick!'

Tess Switched, and the cats scattered into the corners of the room. Lizzie looked at her in concern. 'You's worn out, girl. What's happened?'

Tess flopped, exhausted, into a chair. The seat had been warmed by the cats, and for a long time Tess sat in silence, letting the warmth sink into her and waiting for her strength to return. Lizzie went over to the sink and set about making tea, but she did it quietly, and Tess forgot that she was there until the cup was pressed gently into her hand. She sat up and sipped the sweet tea, but still she could not speak.

'Rat-boy, huh?'

Tess looked up. Above the hob in the fireplace, a

twitching brown nose was poking out of the hole. An unusually long nose. Tears began to pour down Tess's cheeks. Lizzie took off her slipper and threw it at the hole. Long Nose squeaked and disappeared, but a moment later he was back.

'Nanananana,' he said. 'Tail Short Seven Toes curled up with Long Nose and Nose Broken by a Mousetrap. Us guys sleeping. Sun rising, us guys bright eyes, hungry and strong.'

Tess nodded through her tears. 'He's right, Lizzie,' she said. 'You and I can talk in the morning.'

'Off you go, then,' said Lizzie. 'But don't forget to come back to me, will you?'

'Of course not.' Tess gulped down the last of the tea, then put down the cup and Switched. As soon as she was a rat again, she felt better. Rats live together closely, but without attachment or sentiment, and although Kevin's death was still an absence, it was no longer a loss or a cause for grief. She shook herself and began to groom, to put herself back in order, but Lizzie picked her up and lifted her to the hole in the chimney breast before the cats could catch sight of her. There she touched noses with the other two, and quite dispassionately told them her adventures as she followed them through a twisting network of passages and underground tunnels. Long Nose loved the story, and made her tell the bit about the meeting with the first krool again and again, until eventually they arrived at their destination, a snug nest beneath the cowshed. Tess curled up close against Nose Broken by a Mousetrap, and the last thing she heard before she fell asleep was the sound of Nancy above her head, drowsily chewing the cud.

The next morning, Tess made her way back to the

cottage, and, in human form again, told Lizzie everything that had happened. The old woman listened carefully, slapping her knees with delight at each new development in the story. When Tess had finished, they both sat quietly for a few minutes, then Lizzie said, 'If I remembers right, you likes pancakes for breakfast.'

Tess looked over at her in astonishment. 'How can you think about pancakes, Lizzie? Aren't you upset about Kevin?'

'No,' said Lizzie. 'I isn't. There are those who say there's life after death and those who say there isn't. But until I gets there myself, I isn't in any position to say one thing or another.'

'But that isn't the point,' said Tess. 'I'm sad because I won't see him any more.'

'Then you's sad for yourself, girl, not for Kevin.'

Tess looked into the fire. The flames were just taking hold of the wood, leaping up towards the kettle, sending sparks up to disappear into the darkness of the chimney. Lizzie got up and began to crack eggs into a bowl.

'Maybe you're right,' said Tess. 'I don't know. But the thing I can't understand is why it should have been us. I mean, why was I born a Switcher, and Kevin. And you, why you?'

'But all kids is Switchers,' said Lizzie. 'Didn't you know that?'

'What do you mean? How could all kids be Switchers?'

Lizzie began to beat flour into the eggs. 'All kids is born with the ability. But very few learns that they has it. You has to learn before you's eight years old, because after that your mind is set and you takes on the same beliefs as everybody else. A lot of kids find out they can Switch, but when their parents and friends say it's impossible, they believes them instead of theirselves, and then they forgets about it, like they forgets everything that doesn't fit in with what everyone else thinks. It's only a few who has enough faith in theirselves to know that they can do it despite what the rest of the world thinks.'

'So was it all just chance, then? Just coincidence?' Lizzie was beating furiously at her batter. 'Chance?' she said. 'Coincidence? I doesn't know what the words mean.'

A movement in the chimney breast made Tess look up. One crooked nose and four small ones were poking out of the hole, and five pairs of eyes were fixed upon her. 'Grandchildren,' said Nose Broken by a Mousetrap. 'Tail Short Seven Toes telling krools, mammoths, dragons, little ones watching.'

The four small noses quivered in nervous anticipation. Tess laughed and, while Lizzie fried the pancakes, she told her story once again.

Tess's parents were astonished to see her arriving home. They had forgone the chance to escape the weather and flee to southern Europe and had stayed in the seized-up city instead, in case Tess returned. When the snow began to melt and the roads were cleared their hopes rose, but by the time she finally knocked on the door they had almost given up on her. They greeted her with tears and laughter, and there was much talk of forgiveness and all being well that ends well.

But they found it difficult to adjust to the changes that had happened to Tess. Because although the date told her that it had not been so long since she left her bedroom window in the form of an owl, by another reckoning it was a year, a lifetime, an ice age. She could barely remember the child that she had been.

Tess had always been aloof, preferring her own company to that of others, but now it was more than that. She had become a stranger to her parents, and in all the years that followed they never learnt more about her absence than they had heard from Garda Maloney's report. All they knew was that she had been away with a boy, and that she would not or could not discuss the matter. It was clear from her withdrawn behaviour that in some way or other it had ended badly, and they believed that she would tell them about it when she was ready.

So, although they noticed that from time to time Tess wore a silver ring that they had never seen before, they didn't ask her about it. They left her alone and tried to resume the family life of old. Tess tried, too, but it was clear to all of them that she was acting mechanically and not from her heart. She made an effort at school, and succeeded in making one or two friends, but that was mechanical, too, and superficial. It helped to pass the time, but it did nothing to relieve the deep loneliness she felt. Nor did her occasional trips to the park, to join with squirrels or birds or deer for an hour or two. She was not a part of their world, she knew, and nor was she a part of the world of home and school. She was somewhere in between, and all alone.

And her sense of isolation increased whenever she turned on the TV or radio and heard them talking about the famous 'Northern Polar Crisis'. The krools, as she suspected, had retreated back into the ice cap and left no trace of their passing apart from the mysterious barren pathways which stretched for hundreds of miles through the vegetation in the Arctic Circle. A thousand theories were put forward, and it seemed that there was a new one getting aired every week. Each was as ludicrous as the last, but what really made Tess's blood boil was the unanimous agreement that General Wolfe and Scud Morgan were the heroes of the day. And no human being apart from herself and Lizzie would ever know the truth.

Tess's parents never reproached her, but she knew that they had suffered a lot when she disappeared. They didn't try to stop her going for her walks in the park, but they made her promise never to be away for more than two hours and never to go out at night without telling them where she was going. Tess knew that in their terms it was a reasonable request and she agreed. She was sure that in time they would come to trust her again, and she would have more freedom, but in the meantime she would have to live without seeing either Lizzie or her friends the rats.

So she had to look elsewhere for comfort. She saved up her pocket money until she had enough to buy the biggest cage in the pet shop and the nicest white rat they had. Her parents were surprised, because Tess had so often expressed her disapproval of keeping animals in captivity, but they didn't object.

But the rat turned out to be a terrible disappointment. It was terrified of the brown rat that she turned into, and terrified to leave its cage. When she did finally tempt it out into the room, it was timid and clumsy and slow, and no amount of persuasion would bring it to attempt the stairs. The worst of it, though, was that the poor, stupid creature could not even speak Rat. It had been born and brought up in a cage like its parents and grandparents, and it had never been allowed, much less encouraged, to use its intelligence. It had a few basic words-images, but beyond that it was mute, and no effort on Tess's part succeeded in teaching it. The white rat was a mental infant, and would remain that way all its life.

It was company, nonetheless, and quite often Tess would lie awake at night, listening to it exercising itself on the wheel and talking baby-talk while she mulled over her experiences and thought about the decision which would face her in another year or so, when she turned fifteen. Time after time she dreamed of the possibilities, weighing the peaceful lives of dolphins and whales against the briefer but more thrilling lives of rats and goats. Time after time she seemed to reach a satisfactory decision, only to remind herself of how heart-broken her parents would be if she were to disappear from their lives for ever, without explanation. And on a particular night a few days after New Year, she had just reached the point, once again, of deciding to stay human, when something happened that was to make her think all over again, in an entirely different way.

It was the white rat's sudden silence that pulled her out of her reflections and alerted her to the change in the atmosphere. She watched it sniff the air, then turn around and gaze steadily into the darkness outside her window. The hairs prickled on the back of Tess's neck as she got out of bed and crossed warily to the window to look out.

There, on the same tree that the owl had once called from, was the most beautiful bird she had ever seen. It was familiar to her, somehow, and yet she was sure that she had never seen it before, or any other like it. Its bright feathers glowed in the light cast out from her room, and its tail hung down below it, way longer than its body. Then, suddenly, Tess remembered the page of the book where she had seen the bird pictured, and even before she noticed that it had only three toes on its right foot, she knew that it was Kevin. She knew that he had learned, in the nick of time, to find for himself the invisible path which lies between what is and what isn't. As he had fallen, burning, that autumn night which was the eve of his birthday, he had made his final, irreversible Switch, and become the only creature, either of this world or not of it, that could survive that raging fire. And when the helicopters had left the following morning, he had appeared again, rising from his own ashes; a beautiful, golden phoenix.

Tess's heart leapt, racing ahead of her into the night skies where she would soon be flying beside her friend. With a silent apology to her parents for breaking her promise, she reached for the latch and pushed open the window.

If you liked SWITCHERS, then you'll love
MIDNIGHT'S CHOICE.
Here's a thrilling preview to give you the chills . . .

THE STORY CONTINUES...

Tess's concentration was abruptly broken by a loud
scratching noise from Algernon's cage. She turned
and saw him trying to burrow into the corner where
his wheel had been, throwing sawdust all over the
cage and out through the bars.

'Poor old Algernon,' said Tess and then, in Rat,
'Wheel, huh?'

Algernon made no reply, but turned his attention
to another corner of the cage and continued to
scrabble away desperately. It was uncharacteristic
behaviour, and it worried Tess. She picked up the
wheel and began again to unravel the wound-up
paper from around the axle. She had done most of
the work that morning, and it didn't take long to free
it and clear the last few shreds which were draped
between the bars.

'Here you go, Algie. Is this what you want?' Tess
opened the hatch in the top of the cage and reached
in with the wheel in her hand. Before she could
react, before she could even blink, Algernon had run
up the bars of the cage, out through the hatch, and
down Tess's legs to the floor. Tess stared at him in
amazement. She had never seen him behave like that
before. Something must have happened to him. His
timidity was gone, and instead of bumbling round
short-sightedly he was scuttling into the corners of

the room and scratching at the carpet with his claws.

Quickly, Tess refitted the wheel and checked that it was spinning freely. Then she tidied up the floor of the cage, picked the stray shavings out of the foodbowl, and replaced the dirty water with fresh from the tap.

By this time Algernon was at the door, poking his paws into the narrow gap beneath it and gnawing at the wood with his teeth. When Tess reached down to pick him up, he jumped in fright, as though he had been taken by surprise. He had never done that before, either. He wriggled and squirmed as she pushed him through the small door of the cage, and threw himself against it when she closed it. Tess hoped it was the loss of the wheel that had upset him, and that once he found it back in its place he would settle himself down. His behaviour disturbed her more than she liked to admit, and she wondered if she should take him to the vet.

'White rat in pain, huh?' she said to him. 'White rat afraid of sore head? Sore belly?'

Algernon paused in his restless scurrying and looked at her. 'White rat go,' he said, his thought images dim and poorly formed. 'White rat go under city.'

His pictures of the rats' underground system were whimsy, like a young child's drawing of a fairy-tale land. But it was the first time he had used that image, or even given any intimation that he knew such a place existed.

'Brown rats in tunnels,' said Tess. 'Brown rats tough, fierce, biting white rat.'

'White rat go,' said Algernon stubbornly, his restlessness returning. 'White rat go, white rat go, white rat go.' He began to chew with his yellow teeth at the bars of the cage.

Tess sighed. 'Teeth worn down,' she said to him. 'Sunflower seeds won't open, white rat hungry.'

Algernon took no notice whatsoever. Tess returned to the window, but it was impossible for her to relax with the sound of Algernon chewing and scratching and rushing around his cage. Eventually she picked up a book and went downstairs, hoping that he would settle down in her absence. If he was still the same way tomorrow she could bring him to the vet.

Her parents were glad to see her coming down, and her father made room for her on the sofa beside him.

'Everything all right?' he said.

'Just Algernon. He's a bit restless. It's not like him.'

'I expect he needs a pal,' said her mother. 'What about getting another one?'

'As long as it's not female,' said her father. 'There's enough rats in the world as it is without breeding more of them.'

Tess laughed, reassured. The TV programme was humorous, the room was warm, and she had no premonition at all of the dramatic changes that were about to come into her life.

When the evening film was over, Tess brought an apple upstairs to share with Algernon as a bed-time treat. The rat however, had other things on his mind. The room was cold when Tess came into it, and the first thing she did was to go across and close the window. There was no sign of the phoenix beyond it, and she turned her attention to Algernon. He was upside down, hanging by his paws to the wire roof and gnawing on the metal clasp which kept the roof hatch secure. The water bowl had been knocked over again, and almost the entire contents of the cage had been hurled through the bars, littering up the room in a wide circle around the cage. Tess groaned and fought down a desire to punish the white rat. He was already disturbed enough, and scaring him further would not accomplish anything. Far better to try and find out what the problem was.

'Apple, huh?' she said.

In reply, Algernon dropped from the top of the cage, twisting in mid-air so that he landed on his feet, then proceeded to perform the most extraordinary feat of rodent gymnastics, leaping up the sides of the cage, across the roof and down to the floor again in a dizzying sequence of somersaults.

'White rat go, white rat go, white rat go,' he repeated as he swung wildly around.

Tess began to realise that the situation was much more serious than she had thought. It was clear now that the problem wasn't just going to disappear and there was no sense in trying to ignore it. Where did Algernon want to go, and why? She turned his repetitive visual statement into a question and, in reply, Algernon sent a most extraordinary image into her mind.

It was a little like the visual name the city rats had given to Kevin, a gruesome mixture of rat and a rat's conception of a boy. But this new image was vaguer, and tied up with other images as well; wolves perhaps, and bats, all in darkness. Strangest of all, and the most disturbing thing to Tess's human mind, was that this being was calling. It was calling for all the rats in the city to come towards it, and the reason for Algernon's behaviour was suddenly crystal clear. For Tess could tell without any doubt that if she had been a rat at that moment, she would have had no resistance whatsoever to that call.

Switchers 2 – MIDNIGHT'S CHOICE is published by The Bodley Head Children's Books ISBN 0 370 32495 1 Coming soon in paperback from Red Fox!